THE SHARPSHOOTER

JOHN REESE

DOUBLEDAY & COMPANY, INC.

GARDEN CITY, NEW YORK

1974

All the characters in this book
are purely fictional, and any resemblance
to actual persons, living or dead,
is purely coincidental.

Library of Congress Cataloging in Publication Data

Reese, John Henry.
The sharpshooter.

I. Title.
PZ3.R25673Sh [PS3568.E43] 813'.5'4
ISBN: 0-385-08549-4
Library of Congress Catalog Card Number: 74-9045

CHAPTER ONE

The stagecoach teams slowed to a weary walk at the top of the grade. There were only four horses, it was a hot July day, and the coach was badly overloaded. The driver let them loaf, but he looked back nervously over his shoulder.

"Wonder where they went?" he grumbled.

Jefferson Hewitt, riding half asleep beside him, sat up and yawned. "Two men on one horse. They're worse overloaded than we are," he said.

"If they was after me—" the driver said, and left the rest to Hewitt's imagination.

"They don't know what they're after. They're like most of us, creatures of impulse. They don't know what they're going to do until they've done it, and are facing the consequences. We human beings don't really think as often as we say we do. If we did, mankind would not be in the mess it's usually in."

The driver looked back again, this time at the horse haltered to the rear of the stage. Its bridle and a strong, limber lariat were lashed to the saddle horn.

"It's your skin, mister. If I'd lost a horse like that, I'd likely go after him too."

"I had about two hundred and sixty dollars in the pot against him."

"Like to've seen that game."

"It wasn't much. Any fool who loses his head over aces back-to-back isn't a good poker player. Strange thing is, I had figured him to be a good one."

"Mebbe he figgered to get the horse back some other way, and was just bluffing."

"That has been tried too." Hewitt took off his battered old cloth cap, and ran his fingers through his heavy scruff of beard. "How much farther to Kaylee's Ford?"

"Four-five miles. You can see it from the next rise, unless there's too much heat haze. Used to be a real good town, as homey as it was purty. Since the quarry opened up, it's like a damn stampede mining camp. You're going to have trouble finding a room, mister."

"I was thinking of that myself. I think I'll get out at the top of the grade and camp there. Hope you'll forget all about me, however. I need sleep and I don't want to worry all night about being bushwhacked."

"Nobody will know about it from me," the driver said. "I reckon you have your own reasons."

He looked his passenger over, seeing a man of average height, shabbily dressed, with the elbows out of his shirt, and the patches on the knees of his pants almost worn through. Hazel eyes, under bushy brown eyebrows. Probably a short, stiff mustache under those frowzy whiskers. He didn't look like a fugitive, and neither did he look like an ordinary jobless saddle bum.

The driver decided to mind his own business. He let the two teams break into a trot, going down the grade. They slowed to a walk as they started upward. At the top, he reined them in to a stop.

"Hold my leaders," he said to his passenger, "and I'll get your valise out."

Hewitt jumped down and went to the bits of the lead team. The driver got the suitcase out of the boot. He untied the led horse's halter rope and put on the bridle. It was a handsome brown gelding with three white points, and the saddle was a fine one.

The driver had to hold the horse, while Hewitt tied his

suitcase on behind the saddle. The horse was young enough to object to such things, and Hewitt let it object, so long as he had his way in the end. The men inside the coach watched dully. They were all headed for Kaylee's Ford, looking for quarry jobs. All fit the description of good quarrymen—strong backs and weak minds.

Hewitt offered his hand. "The beer is on me, sir, and my thanks for your courtesy," he said.

The driver did not want to take the money hidden in Hewitt's hand, until he saw the glint of gold. It was more than he could resist. "You don't owe me nothing," he grumbled; but he pocketed the gold.

"Why not? You're easy on your passengers and easy on your horses. A master horseman! I like to know the name of a man whose work I respect."

"Earl Godfrey."

"Jefferson Hewitt."

They clasped hands. The driver climbed up to his seat, and shook the lines. The stage was off on its last lap to Kaylee's Ford, where Hewitt now had a friend. It took more than ten dollars to buy a man like Earl Godfrey. Money could only break the ice. You could always find something decent to say about a good man, and Hewitt, more than most men, needed friends.

In every new town, he went out of his way to make friends. Friends could make the difference between success and failure. Someday, they might make the difference between life and death.

"One of us is going to have to yield, Rowdy, so let's get to the point right now," Hewitt said to the horse.

He jumped into the saddle and Rowdy, as he had expected, went up on his hind legs. He had no intention of carrying both man and suitcase. Hewitt let him have one good jump and then pulled him down with a firmness that told the horse it was time to go to work.

Rowdy understood, like the good horse he was, and Hewitt liked him more and more. He had won Rowdy in an all-night poker game that still puzzled him. The idiot who lost his judgment over aces back-to-back, when the horse was in the pot, had not played like an idiot most of the night. He had not been drunk. He just had not played the hand that counted, like the poker player he had seemed to be.

Hewitt turned the horse off the narrow road, and Rowdy grunted as he went gamely up the steep slope toward the pines. Hewitt had seen the glint of a little spring-fed creek up there. By the time the horse reached it, it had lost interest in the suitcase behind the saddle.

I'll have to watch myself with you, you rascal, Hewitt thought. . . . He dared not get attached to a horse. Sooner or later, there was always a parting. He dared not get attached to people, either, in his line of work.

Hewitt unsaddled the horse and let it drink. He picked a campsite a hundred feet from the spring and left the suitcase, bridle, and saddle there. He put Rowdy's halter rope on the end of the lariat and found a dead branch for the other end. Rowdy could drag it, but not far, and not fast.

Hewitt had to hurry to get back down to the road then. He squatted on his heels, cap off, in the brush above it. An Indian or a dog would have detected him; but two tired poker players, with only one horse between them, would surely be less acute.

He could hear them arguing long before he saw them. The one called "Mac" was riding. "Toby," the former owner of Rowdy, limped along afoot, hanging to the saddle for help. They stopped to rest where Hewitt had left the stage. Neither man noticed the signs in the dirt of Hewitt's departure from the stage.

Mac got down stiffly. His was just a so-so horse, but he

took good care of it. He loosened the saddle and lifted the bridle headstall to let in cool air.

"How's your feet, Toby?" he said.

"They hurt like hell, what you think?" Toby growled. "I got to get my horse back."

"You ain't going to get him back."

"You watch me!"

"All you'll do is get in trouble, you fool around with that Pinkerton. End up in the stockade, that's what you'll do."

Toby took off his hat and mopped the sweat out of it. "Well, that wouldn't be no worse than breaking and loading rock for a nickel a ton."

"Remember old Shepherdson? He used to work in a quarry. He said you could really make the money, once you got onto it."

"If you got no more brains than Shepherdson, I reckon a quarry is good duty. But not for me. All I want is to get my horse back and get the hell out of here."

"You ain't going to get that horse back, so you might as well get used to it."

They argued sociably, like old friends. Both were in their forties—tall men, raw-boned, hard-faced, tough. By their erect bearing, he was sure that both were Army deserters, old-timers who had walked out while drunk. Now both wished they had done their ten days, instead of being posted for desertion.

The peacetime Army was built on such capable dregs, as Hewitt could testify, having served in it himself. Toby and Mac were not the worst specimens he had ever met. Should war break out, they would become officers overnight, trainers of the volunteer Army on which the Republic depended.

In peacetime, nobody wanted them. Toby and Mac both wore .45 revolvers in cheap, mail-order holsters; the

guns were probably Army issue, the holsters, bad camou-
flage. They started on the way to Kaylee's Ford again,
Toby riding this time, Mac taking his turn afoot. The last
thing Hewitt heard came from Mac:

"*You* give your horse away, and *I'm* the one afoot now.
And what did you get out of it? Nary a damn thing!"

In a way, it confirmed Hewitt's suspicions that Toby had
deliberately lost his fine horse last night. Hewitt returned
thoughtfully to his suitcase. He sat down in the shade,
opened it, and took out a small package wrapped in butcher
paper, and a collapsible metal cup. Both had been bought
in the Nebraska range town where he had played poker
last night and caught the northbound stage this morning.

No man liked comfort better than Jefferson Hewitt, but
no man stood discomfort better. He feasted on summer
sausage and cold spring water, meanwhile studying another thing that did not make sense. This was a letter,
taken from his suitcase, and dated a month ago, in Kaylee's
Ford, South Dakota:

Mr. J. Hewitt, Esq., Dear Sir:

    You said call on you if ever I needed help. No
man ever needed it worse than I. You owe me nothing.
It is a man's duty to testify to the truth, not a favor
to anyone. That is how I am. Nevertheless, I
would appreciate your very valuable help.

    Have been dep. U. S. marshal some time here in
Kaylee's Ford, so named because Capt. Elmo J. Kaylee,
of the 7th, stood off the Sioux for 15 hours, with 9
men armed only with side arms. This heroic tradition
gives the community a spirit I would hate to betray.
Otherwise, I do not care to confide details of my
problem to paper.

    It cost me $21.38 in telegrams to your office in
Cheyenne, seeking your present address. As you

know, I am a poor man. From this you may infer how badly I need you. I recall your skills with immense respect, and hesitate less to impose upon you because I looked forward so much to seeing you in action.

Sincerely your obdt. svt.,

R. E. Lee Stambaugh

His strongest memory of Lee Stambaugh was of a man impossible to understand. This letter only added to the confusion. *It does not make sense,* Hewitt thought, *and winning the horse from Toby doesn't, either. Nothing about this whole deal makes any damn sense. . . .*

He thought back to Colorado, almost three years ago, an extradition hearing in the governor's office where a five-thousand-dollar fee was at stake. Hewitt had already spent more than twelve hundred dollars on expenses.

He had found his man, but proving he was the right one, to the satisfaction of the state of Colorado, turned out to be a muddle. The governor had his legal secretary conduct a formal extradition hearing. The crucial part of Hewitt's testimony went something like this:

Governor's Secretary: But he was drunk, was he not, when he confessed to this crime?
Hewitt: Correction, please, sir. He did not confess, he boasted, and it happened not once, but five times. On two of those occasions, he might have been slightly intoxicated, but not on the other three.
Governor's Secretary: My dilemma is this: I'm inclined to believe you, but the man is a hard drinker, you have hunted him down for a handsome fee, and he says that you bought him whiskey. This brings in the possibility of entrapment, by which government is loathe to profit.

Hewitt: It wasn't a problem of entrapping him, but of shutting him up. I realize that it's my word against his, but—

At this point, a man stood up in the audience and asked to be heard. Hewitt lost heart when he recognized Lee Stambaugh, a cross-grained, short-tempered deputy sheriff who had no use for private detectives. A lean, fit, clean-shaven, neatly dressed man about Hewitt's own age, he took more pride in his enemies than most men did in their friends. The governor's secretary obviously was not one of his friends:

Governor's Secretary: This is a formal hearing, Mr. Deputy, so unless what you have to say is relevant—
Stambaugh: It's relevant. Put me under oath, and I will testify that Mr. Hewitt did not have to get this fellow drunk. He's drunk most of the time. He did not have to entrap him, either. As Mr. Hewitt said, he boasted of the crime, and I know because I overheard him to do it on two occasions.
Governor's Secretary: I see. How did it happen that you overheard the said boasting?
Stambaugh: I was investigating Mr. Hewitt. I have not got much respect for fly-cops, and when one comes into my jurisdiction, I want to know what brings him here. It is a duty, not a pleasure, to testify that he has the right man. I only hope His Excellency signs the extradition writ so we can be rid of both of them.

The moon came up, and Hewitt lay staring at it sleeplessly, trying to remember the enigmatic Mr. Stambaugh better. He recalled giving Stambaugh his card, and at the same time, complimenting him on the detective work that had made it possible for him to testify. Hewitt had had no idea that Stambaugh was within hearing.

"I probably will never need your help," Stambaugh said coldly, putting the card carefully in his wallet, "and I do hope to God I don't. But a little humility is good for us all, and if that time comes, Mr. Hewitt, you may be sure you will hear from me. Now, please take your prisoner and get the hell out of Colorado."

In all his lonesome years as a detective, Hewitt had never felt quite so lonesome as now. He was already tired to death, having run an endless case down in Cherry County, Nebraska. There, Stambaugh's letter had caught up with him.

Now, instead of taking the rest he had promised himself for a year and a half, he was off on another job in which there was not even a fee in sight. It was well after midnight when Hewitt finally removed his boots and put them under his head for a pillow. He spread a handkerchief out beside his head, and put his .45 on it. He was used to sleeping on the .32 he wore in a shoulder holster.

He awakened, little refreshed, at daylight. He breakfasted scantily on the last of the summer sausage and all the cold, delicious water he wanted. He caught and saddled Rowdy, and after a slight argument with the horse, got the suitcase tied on behind the saddle again.

Thirty minutes later, Kaylee's Ford, South Dakota, was in sight. He liked its looks the moment he saw it. There was good cattle range around here, but the town had grown up in the confluence of several shallow canyons, with trees everywhere. The railroad had cut a raw slash straight through it less than ten years ago.

He entered by the stage road, seeing the new county courthouse on a grade that sloped down from the road, to

his left, half a block away. To his right were several frame
buildings already going to seed. The stage depot occupied
the first of them with its stable next door.

Next came a big, ramshackle saloon, ambitiously named
the Little Bighorn Battlefield Men's Saloon. And next to
it was a doorway, leading to an upper floor. From the up-
stairs windows leaned, even at this early hour, the be-
draggled women who followed the railroads and plied their
ancient profession everywhere.

Hewitt saw blanket Indians, and Indians in the white
man's garb. He saw immigrant Irishmen, Swedes, Germans,
and Slavs on the street in the quarryman's dusty jeans and
leather aprons. He saw not one man who looked like a
ranch hand or cattleman, although there were big cattle
stockyards near the railroad.

Cowboys and cattlemen are outnumbered by the rock
heads from the quarry, Hewitt decided. They won't come
to town until they can all come at once, and they'll be
armed like the Royal Fusiliers. . . .

A man with a red flannel armband around his arm came
out of the Battlefield Saloon. Vigilante? The armband
would indicate this, and so did the man's inquisitive
hostility. Hewitt ignored him and rode on.

Kaylee's Ford had grown up spoke-fashion, all its streets
radiating from a forked main road where all these canyons
seemed to come together. He had come into town on one
fork of a Y. At its crotch, he could see the creek crossing
the road a block ahead of him.

Just beyond the creek, he could see the heavy, four-horse
dump wagons of the quarry, and beyond that road, the
raised fill of the railroad. Looking back over his shoulder,
at the other fork of the Y, he saw one of the prettiest little
tree-shaded towns in his experience.

Just then he heard the deep, echoing *boom* . . .
boom . . . *boom* . . . of dynamite shots at the quarry. No

one in Kaylee's Ford could ever forget the change that had
come over their town, as long as it was shaken by those
blasts several times a day.

He held Rowdy down to a prancing walk, and in a moment was crossing the creek at a shallow ford with a flat
rock bottom. This, no doubt, was where the legendary
Captain Kaylee had stood off the Sioux. At the deeply
rutted road that ran parallel to the creek, he sat his horse
a minute and watched the high-wheeled, four-horse quarry
wagons pass.

They were all dump-bottom wagons, holding perhaps
three tons. They had a downhill pull while loaded, and
returned empty up a slight grade. He turned Rowdy and
followed a wagon to the railroad. Here, the four horses had
to put their bellies down and dig in to haul the wagon up
the ramp to an elevated loading dock.

A man stood by to hit the trip without stopping the
horses. The rock cascaded out of the wagon and down a
chute into a railroad gondola car, spotted below it. There
seemed to be a wagon unloading about every ninety
seconds—a big, efficient, well-run operation, beyond question.

Hewitt followed an empty wagon to the quarry, the size
of which surprised him. Three big tunnels had been driven
back into the cliff. Nearby, on a flat, stood the big tents—
one where the cooks worked and the men ate, two where
the men bunked, one for an office, shop, and harness-
maker's repair bench.

Hewitt whistled softly; there must be at least five hundred men working here. And there was an old saying that
hard rock called for hard men. Having worked a week or two
in a quarry himself, Hewitt could not help respecting the
man—whoever he was—who was holding all this hard-
driven, fast-moving organization together.

Narrow-gauge tracks vanished into the black night of the

tunnels. Horse-drawn cars kept moving out with loads, returning with empties after the loads had been dumped into the wagons at another elevated dock.

"You! Looking for someone, cowboy?"

Hewitt turned. It was more than a foreman. A man at least six feet three was looking down his nose at him. It was the strong, arrogant nose of a man born rich, and his accent was the arrogant one of the American educated in England. Blue eyes like chips of granite. Mouth like an unhealed stab wound. Those laced, high boots were the mark of the dude everywhere west of the Missouri.

Hewitt made Rowdy prance a little, and made a small, polite bow. "Just looking," he said, smiling.

"You're trespassing."

"Well, if I must, I'll plead guilty to that and go. But you're damned inhospitable."

He turned and made Rowdy prance. The man's voice came again.

"Hold it! Let's see that horse of yours."

Hewitt turned Rowdy. "As you like."

"How old is he?"

"Five-year teeth not quite in. Must have been foaled in the winter."

"How much do you want for him?"

"This horse? Oh, he's not for sale!"

"Nonsense! Everything is for sale," the man said brusquely. "What's your price for him?"

"That's where we differ. To me, not everything has a price. By the time you're old enough to have learned manners, maybe you'll know that too."

Rowdy loved to show off. Hewitt turned on and let him go up on the bit, giving this overbearing quarryman a view of his hind end. Which should give him an idea of how both Hewitt and his horse felt.

CHAPTER TWO

He saw no sign of Mac and Toby, which did not surprise
him. The two were not likely to make themselves conspicuous. He did count five men—all on foot—wearing red
armbands. By their dress, they were townsmen, and not
particularly excited about the job of volunteer peace officer.

They looked him over carefully, but none spoke to him.
Just another saddle bum, they probably decided. He saw
one quarryman with his arm in a sling, his crushed hand
heavily bandaged. He was in no pain, however, having been
drinking hard. Hewitt reined Rowdy in beside him and
struck up a conversation.

"Smashed a hand, I see."

"Yeah. Want to see it? I got it all wrapped up, but I
don't mind showing it to you."

"I've seen smashed hands before. It's a hard life we
quarrymen lead."

"Yes, sir! Takes a hard man to stay with it. But I'll be
back there, making little ones out of big ones in three or
four days."

"I bet you will. Where is all this rock going?"

"A new fill on the line, about twenty miles west of here.
Railroad's got nigh three hundred men there."

"How many quarrymen and teamsters here?"

"Close to six hundred, when everybody's working."

Another series of dynamite shots went *boom* . . .
boom . . . *booming* through the air. Rowdy became un-

easy, as the ground shivered beneath him. The injured quarryman suddenly began walking rapidly away.

A fat, slattern woman wearing a filthy apron had come to the door of a restaurant and was looking at the quarryman truculently. In the restaurant window was a sign, ROCK HEADS NOT WELCOME HERE. Hewitt walked Rowdy to a scrubby softwood tree that grew beside the cafe, tied him, and went inside.

"Too late for breakfast, too early for dinner," the woman said.

"I'm at your mercy, ma'am. Starved to death, and I smelled something so good that I followed it a mile, to here. Isn't there something you can serve me?" Hewitt said.

She pointed to the sign in the window. Hewitt turned on all his considerable charm: "Surely you can tell a cattleman from a quarry rock head! I've heard of your cooking as far away as the Texas Panhandle. I forget your name, but they say your cooking is unforgettable."

She thawed slightly. "Myra Green. My husband was Lonnie Green. We used to work for the Rocker W, in the Panhandle. He was the foreman and—"

"And you were the cook. That's the name, all right, Myra. Lonnie passed away, I understand."

Lonnie had, indeed; Myra told him of the tragedy, the rapid hardening of her husband's liver, symptom by symptom. Meanwhile, she fried a steak and three eggs. It was not a very good meal, but it was filling.

She put a ticket down beside him with a glare that dared him to object to the seventy-five-cent bill. He put a silver dollar on it and asked her for another cup of coffee. She brought it. She was his friend for life.

They chatted as he drank it. "Fellow by the name of Harvey something—is he still sheriff here?"

"Nobody by that name was ever sheriff here, that I know of."

"That's odd. What's the sheriff's name?"

"Ain't got none. It used to be Fred Gerard, but he got killed the first day the quarry was open. County only paid forty a month, and Fred had a family to support. Killed in a rock slide, poor durned fool."

"I see. Who keeps the peace now?"

"Two federal deppity marshals."

He raised an eyebrow. "Two of them?"

"Yes. Stambaugh's the boss, but he won't be for long. People won't stand for it. They like Shane better."

"What seems to be the trouble?"

"The Patterson murder, that's what," she said, gloomily yet with a certain air of excitement.

"Stambaugh can't solve the mystery?"

"No mystery to it. He's got the man who done it. Folks would've had him strung up long ago, only Stambaugh won't stand for it. Listen, why do you need a trial for a big rock-head brute that raped and killed a twelve-year-old girl? Why should the taxpayers have to feed him until some judge has the guts to come in here and sentence him to hang? One of these nights, people will just get plain fed up, and they'll shoot their way in and take this murderer out and hang him and then burn the tree down. And if Stambaugh gets in the way, too bad for him!"

Ah yes, Stambaugh indeed had a problem. . . . "What about the men with the red armbands, Myra?"

"They're Stambaugh's citizen guards. Bunch of old law-and-order poops that'll hide under the bed, if they ever storm that jail. Sorry, mister, but I got to get back to my kitchen and get ready for the noon rush."

"I wonder if I could leave a suitcase here until I find myself a place to stay?"

She showed him where to put it behind the counter. He

brought it in, and gave her another fifty cents for keeping an eye on it. She brought him another cup of coffee, and he sat drinking it and wondering whether to give Stambaugh a hand, or merely ride quietly out of town.

I'll stay, he decided. Damned if I can stand a lynching. Besides, I like the looks of this town. Or what this town was before the quarry came here. Hell, I wanted a vacation, didn't I? Stopping a lynching party could give me a whole new outlook on life. . . .

The man who called himself Jefferson Hewitt had come out of the Missouri Ozarks and into the Army, as a teen-age boy who could barely sign his name. He had never had a whole dollar in his hands, but those same hands had a deadly skill with rifle, six-gun, or knife, even then.

Six years later, he had educated himself to where he was that most valuable of soldiers, a noncom who could relieve the regimental officers of most of their daily work. He never rose higher than corporal, but he was the pet of every sergeant he worked for.

After the Army, he had worked five years for the Pinkerton agency. A loner, restless and curious, he never minded the contempt people displayed when he was revealed as a detective. No one liked a detective, particularly one who demanded big fees and, as a consequence, worked for rich men.

He had an orderly mind that had been sharpened by Army life, and he had nerve and judgment far beyond his years. When he quit his Pinkerton job, it was because he could have more money and independence as a partner in his own agency.

Now, for ten years, he had been one of the owners of Bankers' Bonding & Indemnity Company—B.B. & I.—of Cheyenne, Wyoming. It was a highly respected firm, with an enviable reputation among banks and other well-heeled clients of detective agencies.

Hewitt did the detective work. His partner, Conrad Meuse, was a tight-fisted German immigrant who had once taught philosophy in a German university. He had got out of Germany two jumps ahead of the police, to whom he had been a dangerous revolutionary. Either the German cops had been 180° wrong, or experience had wrought a profound change of heart in Conrad. He was now the most reactionary man Hewitt had ever known.

Conrad wrote the bonds for public and corporation officials and kept the partnership books. The two had only one thing in common—a good, healthy greed for money. B.B. & I. did not work cheaply. After each case was closed, Hewitt and Conrad quarreled bitterly over the division of the profits. Hewitt was a genius at padding an expense account, Conrad a brutal brandisher of the red pencil.

It was a wholly satisfactory partnership, and how Conrad was going to sputter, when he heard that Hewitt was working for nothing here in Kaylee's Ford! In fact, he was probably sputtering already, wondering where Hewitt was.

Jefferson Hewitt used other names—in fact, his real name was so far in the past that the kid who had worn it seemed no longer to belong to Hewitt. He changed personalities whenever he changed names for a job. He had come to like Jefferson Hewitt better than any of his other working names—Aaron B. London, Zeke Harvey, Alec Laidlaw, Richard Bing, W. A. Chastain, and Reuben Whitman. Over the years, he had grown to fit Jefferson Hewitt, until only that name now fit him.

Hewitt had friends throughout the nation. Some of them knew him by only one name—others, by several. He could count on his friends for help, because he had never failed in the universal measure of mutual respect—money.

He did not fling money about, but he paid well and promptly for whatever he needed.

Hewitt could have retired long ago, Conrad Meuse being the cautious investment genius that he was. By most standards, Hewitt was a rich man.

He kept on working because he enjoyed the excitement and risk of his job. He kept on working because anyone likes being the best—and that was his reputation, the best there was in his field, especially in the rugged and sometimes dangerous West.

He worked because manhunting fed his restless hunger for new places, new people, new excitement. He kept working because it was a solitary job, and he was still a loner.

When Hewitt went to New York, Philadelphia, or Washington on business, colleagues treated him with respect. No one looked upon him as countrified. But they refused to play poker with him, and did not introduce him to their daughters or (sometimes) their wives.

Hewitt could have made a good living as a gambler. He understood the mathematics of odds and had made a study of luck, which often made idiots of mathematicians. He was also a student of human personality, which played so strong a part in "streaks," winning or losing.

He could not explain it, but he knew how men often made and lost their luck, simply by being the men they were. He faced the fact that his winning streak had been prolonged beyond the average and must someday end. All streaks came to an end, and until his did, he would bet his stack on himself, as he always had.

Hewitt spoke several languages workably. He got on well with both men and women. He was a better shot than when he had come out of the Ozarks. He had also taken pains to see that his reputation exceeded his abilities. He was good, all right; but no man on earth could shoot as well as the Jefferson Hewitt of living legend.

Hewitt was unscrupulous with unscrupulous men, a bully with bullies, and impatient with stupidity. At times he was an unforgiving enemy. But being right most of the time had given him a tolerance that made it possible for him to be generous with forgiveness sometimes too.

He loved money and excitement, but he was cool in a crisis. There were some jobs he would not do, and every now and then turned down a fat job because it violated his rubbery code of ethics.

He liked most of the things about his life. And perhaps the thing he liked best was being Jefferson Hewitt. There's an advantage to creating your own name, and your own personality to go with it. He was fairly sure that a loving and tolerant Creator would understand.

Hewitt stood up at the restaurant counter, and lifted his cup for one last swallow of coffee.

He put it down quickly as he saw, across the street, a man who looked only too familiar. He went swiftly to the door, but remained back a foot or two from it. He could see clearly from here, but the screen door kept him invisible from the sunny street.

It was Toby across the street, and he had not noticed the horse tied to the tree outside the cafe. Toby had just come out of a small grocery store and was looking irresolutely up the street.

Hewitt inched closer to the screen door. Now he could see the other deserter, Mac, just as he came out of another store, three or four doors away.

The two did not look at each other, but Mac shrugged hopelessly, and somehow Toby caught the signal and shook his head with the same air of despair.

Hewitt chuckled silently. The two might as well have shouted their intentions to him. Toby and Mac were looking for a quick, easy, safe, cheap stickup that would yield a little eating money. The exchange of signals had meant that the places each had just investigated did not suit the purpose.

What they wanted was a small place, run by an old man, a woman, or kids. They did not plan to use guns. One swing of a fist to put a storekeeper out of action. One grab at the cash drawer and off they would go. It was poor pay, but the petty robber who stuck to his trade usually outlived the colorful two-gun bandits who robbed banks and trains and Army payrolls.

Hewitt could see Rowdy clearly. The horse had turned his rump to the building, covering his back with the leaves of the tree. Safe from the flies, he had put his head down to doze.

Still without noticing the horse, Toby and Mac went into two other stores. Mac came out at once, looking downcast. A moment later, Toby came out of a small store that was straight across from the restaurant. He nodded. The two sauntered closer to each other.

They stopped a yard apart, and still did not look at each other. Only someone who knew what he was watching for could have suspected they were talking things over. Hewitt could imagine what they were saying:

No luck! (This from Mac.) Everything was wrong with the place I was in.

The one I was in is just right. (This from Toby.) Here's what it's like, and here's how we'll work it. . . .

A long, serious discussion between two men who did not even look at each other. Then they turned, as though to just "happen" to walk into the store together.

That was when Toby saw Rowdy. He caught Mac by the arm. He pointed. More heated discussion, Mac shaking his head, Toby arguing stubbornly.

It was Toby who had his way. He tore himself free and

started across the street. Mac followed sadly. Toby took hold of Rowdy's bit ring and turned the horse out from under his fly guard of green leaves.

"I told you, goddam it, this was my horse!" he said.

"All right, the hell with you, then," said Mac. "Go ahead and get yourself in trouble! You ain't going to get that damn fly-cop after me."

"We need two horses, don't we?"

"What we need is something to eat, Toby. I'm so hungry, I'm shaking like a rattlesnake's rattles."

"We'll get the money. But then we're going to take this horse along with us. He's mine, and that damn feller cheated me out of him!"

Hewitt unbuttoned his coat and dropped his hand on his .45. It lay in a holster that he had designed himself, one that fit inside the waistband of his pants, in a position so close to horizontal it would almost fall into his hand. The two now had their backs to him. He opened the screen door quietly and stepped outside.

"Tin-*shun!*" he shouted.

They came rigidly erect, eyes rolling wildly. Hewitt thumbed the horse out of the way to let them see his hand on his gun. Mac seemed about ready to burst into tears, but Toby only got red-faced. His eyes rolled more wildly, as he recognized Hewitt.

"At ease, troops," Hewitt said.

"You dirty, double-crossing son of a bitch!" Toby said, almost in a whimper.

"Now, why do you want to talk to me like that?" said Hewitt. "You're not thinking very well, boys."

"About what?" Mac said, stupidly.

"About coshing somebody in that store, grabbing a few pence, and then stealing my horse. Don't you boys see what you're up against in this town? It's ready to blow up in a lynching party, and if it happens, everybody that gets in the way will get strung up."

"I want my horse," Toby said, with the beautiful simplicity of the stubbornly stupid.

Toby had tobacco and papers in his shirt pocket. Hewitt helped himself to them and rapidly twisted a cigarette. He knew Toby was measuring his chances of beating him to the draw, but he could watch Toby's hands while making his cigarette, and he knew when Toby decided it was a losing proposition.

"*My* horse, Toby," Hewitt said, smiling as he lighted the cigarette. He put the makin's back in Toby's pocket. "Get this straight—try to lay hands on that horse, and I'll kill you, and you'll only be Number Seven. I would hate to have to kill you, Toby. I like you boys, I really do."

"Why?" said Mac.

"I've been up against it myself. Boys, let me stake you to a meal and a few dollars. Then, either get out of town, or make up your minds to picking up a stake by working in the quarry. Listen to the advice of a friend! Do you want the civil law on your tails as well as the provost marshal? This wouldn't be ten days in the stockade, you know. You're talking about life in prison!"

Hewitt was a persuasive talker who played his rich, baritone voice like a pipe organ. Their desperate rage crumpled before his earnest insincerity. He was not sure why he bothered to make friends of them, unless it was that he wanted to keep Rowdy without complicating his job here with their enmity.

He steered them into the restaurant. "Myra, I want you to meet some good friends of mine, Toby and Mac. Boys, this is Mrs. Green," he said.

The two smelled nice, rich, greasy food, and fell under the charms of the woman who cooked it. Both snatched off their hats.

"Parmenter's the name, ma'am, Toby Parmenter."

"Willie MacAdams, ma'am. I'm called Mac."

"It's my treat, Myra," said Hewitt. "Let's see how much these two can eat, what do you say?"

He talked to them in a low voice while they wolfed their meal. A nickel a ton was really good pay, once a man got toughened to it. Why, Hewitt himself had turned out fifty tons a day, and they were both bigger, stronger men. Mac was the easier of the two to convince. Toby held out, until Hewitt offered each man a five-dollar bill.

"We old soldiers must stick together. This will keep you, until you get a payday. What more can I do?"

"You can give me back my horse," said Toby.

"Subject closed, my friend. He's *my* horse."

Toby gave a final belch, got up off the stool, wiped his mouth on his sleeve, and pointed his trigger finger at Hewitt. "You cheated me out of that horse, and you better take good care of him until I get him back. I'll go work in your goddam quarry because what else can I do? But one of these days, gumshoe—*one of these days—!*"

Hewitt put down three dollars for Myra, and took the two deserters by the arm and steered them toward the door. "That's why I like you boys so much," he said. "You don't change your minds every time the wind changes, do you?"

CHAPTER THREE

He hailed an elderly man wearing a red armband: "Where might I find the United States marshal, sir?"

"Sheriff's office, basement of the courthouse," the man replied. "What do you want with him?"

"An old friend."

The man's face lighted up. "You the detective he sent for? Pleased to meet you, Mr. Hewitt. My name is Kirby, Tom Kirby. It's an honor to shake your hand!"

"You have heard of me?"

"Lord-*ee*, Mr. Hewitt, everybody has heard of you! And we sure do need you. Lynching just purely goes against my grain. It's something a town never lives down, I've found. And the thing is, the way people are worked up here, if you're *against* lynching, you're *for* rape and murder."

"That's the way the miserable human creature is constituted, sir. I don't know what we can do to prevent a lynching, but we'll certainly give it a try, won't we?"

But he felt an immense weariness come over him as he walked Rowdy through hostile streets toward the courthouse. The old man had demonstrated one thing—that this case, though a change, was not going to be a rest. And how he needed a rest! For perhaps three years, his life had been a kaleidoscopic progression of uncomfortable trains, rickety stagecoaches, bone-jarring horses; of sleepless nights, bad food, and one brainless showdown after another with stubborn, ignorant, avaricious men in whom the streak of human nobility was conspicuous by its absence.

This would have been a good time for a trip into the Black Hills, or perhaps Canada. Kill my own meat, he thought. Cook it over my own fire, when I feel like it, not because the clock tells me to. How I need to rest!

But no use blaming Robert E. Lee Stambaugh. Had Hewitt returned to Cheyenne, Conrad Meuse would have talked him into going out on another case somehow, somewhere.

He put off going to the courthouse, to give the town a good look at him and his horse. Passing again the restaurant where he had eaten and had fed Toby and Mac, he happened to glance at the store Toby had approved for a cheap stickup.

A white figure—or part of one—crossed the small window. He thought it had the contour of a woman's bust, a proud bust, a magnificent one. He tied Rowdy in front of the store, and went inside. The sign on the screen door said: SEWING SHOP. YARD GOODS, BUTTONS, NEEDLES, THREAD, & ALL NEEDLEWORK SUPPLIES.

His instincts had not misled him. She was just emerging from the shadows of a back room, carrying several heavy bolts of cloth. He yanked off his cap and tried not to stare. He flung the cap on the counter and went behind it, to take her burden of cloth from her.

"Where shall I put them, ma'am? No woman should carry such a load," he said.

"I've carried heavier, but thank you," she replied, coolly. "On the shelf there, if you please."

He put the cloth on the shelf and hastened to get back on the other side of the counter. She looked at him with not a little suspicion in her eyes.

"Now, how may I help you?" she said.

"I came to help you, ma'am," he said. "Where do you

keep your cash? In an unsafe place, I'm afraid. You were almost robbed, ma'am, a few moments ago."

That caught her off guard. "I was *what?*"

"Robbed, ma'am."

He could carry on a conversation and miss nothing with his eyes. Not a girl—probably about thirty. Great masses of light brown hair, put up in a fashion to frame her face perfectly. Brown eyes, large and wide apart, met his with neither boldness nor coquetry. Big, wide, full mouth, both sensitive and passionate if Hewitt knew women's mouths. And he thought he did.

Not one of your lithe and spindly women. Big, and proud of it. Wide of hip, straight-backed, strong. She was chastely and simply dressed, in a black skirt and a white waist with a high collar. If the collar was meant to mitigate the impact of her bosom, it failed. The only word that occurred to Hewitt was statuesque.

"There was a man in here, a few moments ago, ma'am?"

"Yes. He wanted to buy a shirt. He thought—"

"Excuse me, ma'am, but he didn't think anything of the kind. He was not interested in a shirt. He found out, I'm sure, where you kept your cash."

"Why, when I told him this wasn't a clothing store, he asked if I could change a ten-dollar gold piece. I had to look in the till to say I couldn't."

She opened a simple money drawer, set in her side of the counter. An old saloon fighter like Toby could have floored her with a short, soundless jab. He would have had her money and been gone in one minute.

"Better find another place for it, ma'am. Mustn't make it easy for people to rob you."

She became very pale, and her fingertips went to her temples. "I see. Thank you. I—I might have expected a robbery. It's all that has been omitted so far."

"Headache, ma'am?"

"It's nothing. There's no excuse for it, and yet at the slightest crisis lately, my head just bursts. It is so annoying, when I'm so healthy."

"Pure neuralgia, ma'am. A warning that if you let your worries mean too much, you may become neurasthenic, which would be too bad. Put your elbows on the desk, and lean your forehead in your hands."

Without thinking, she obeyed. His fingertips found the knots of a muscle in spasm, in the back of her neck. He traced the spasm down the spinal column to the last cervical vertebra. Meanwhile he was saying:

"I learned this technique from a physician, who had it from a Chinese expert in India. Unfortunately, I had to send the good doctor to jail, because he was more skillful at manipulating distorted muscles than at manipulating corporation ledgers.

"Now, see if you don't feel better, ma'am."

"Why, how wonderful!" She blinked at him incredulously. "The ache is all gone!"

"Yes, ma'am. I urge you to move your cash drawer. Save yourself some trouble later, and perhaps danger too."

Her lovely face became unhappy. "I shall, but the way things are going here, it may not matter."

"Is business so bad? I should think the quarry would bring prosperity to Kaylee's Ford."

"They don't buy needlework things," she said, bitterly. "I did well in the spring, when I first opened the shop. Now the ladies of the town are afraid to walk the streets without their husbands."

"The quarrymen?"

"Yes. The wagon road is so close, and the quarry management does nothing to restrain the men."

"I should think the management would want to get along with the townspeople."

She said angrily, "Why? They'll be gone when winter

closes in. They're like an occupying army! They're changing the very character of the town. It was so lovely here until they came! Such good, warm, friendly people, but now they're all vindictive and hateful too. And all so men may take stone from the ground!"

She was stirring him more than he liked to be stirred, threatening his lone-wolf independence. He picked his cap up off the counter, gave her a smile and a small bow.

"Don't give up hope, ma'am. It takes time to work these things out. It may be good again here."

He went out, and she did not thank him again for relieving her headache. She surely felt a little guilty about that, or perhaps she had been stirred and stimulated by it, and that was why she felt guilty. The thought pleased Hewitt.

There was a barber shop in the same block. On impulse, he went in and paid a dollar for the place of the next man up. He had a hair cut and a shave, and had his short, stiff mustache trimmed. Listening to the voices of the quarrymen waiting their turns, he understood why the good women of Kaylee's Ford felt unsafe on the streets. The woman in the sewing shop had called them an occupying army. She's right, he thought—the Huns who occupied Rome. . . .

He took a canter up the quarry road, which seemed to be the key to the problem. About halfway between the ford and the quarry, a high rock fill had been put in, where a small creek had once crossed the road. Now it no longer flowed into the big creek, and a stagnant pond had formed on the upstream side of the fill.

No one would ever lie awake here again, listening to the music of water tumbling down the rocks from the spring. Bears and small boys would no longer fish the pools here. He heard the *boom . . . boom . . . boom . . . boom* of another cluster of dynamite shots in the quarry, and saw how it rippled the stagnant scum that floated on the water.

It was too high a price to pay, even for a railroad. Well, it was time to run Lee Stambaugh down, and see where one unimportant but impatient detective fit into the tense scheme of things here.

Behind the courthouse, on the downhill side, stood a stable and a corral, on which a sign identified them as property of the sheriff. The sheriff's sign was over the door in what was practically the basement of a courthouse built into a lot that sloped more steeply than it had seemed to, from the road.

The door opened into a big public office, empty. Hewitt went through a door in the wooden wall at the rear, and found himself in a short, wide corridor. The wood, he saw, was merely a sheathing over heavy steel bars. To his left was an open door.

He looked inside and saw a big, comfortable room with two cots in it, a half-underground room that would be cool in the summer and warm in the winter. There was more wood sheathing over the steel bars of the corridor.

To his right, he could see two large cells. There was also a door, almost at his hand. He opened it and found himself in a small office where a fattish, youngish man sat at a desk with his plump cheeks in his hands, while he read a frayed newspaper dreamily. He did not look up, even when Hewitt tapped lightly on the desk with his knuckles.

"I'm looking for Lee Stambaugh," Hewitt said.

After a moment, the fat youth condescended to say without bothering to look up, "He ain't here. Are you blind, or what?"

"When do you expect him?"

Fatty still did not look up, but he reached behind him for a new straw Panama planter's hat. He put it on his head and cocked it forward. Now he could not possibly see

Hewitt. From a battered tin can on the desk, he fished a half-smoked cigar. He stuck it in his mouth, but did not bother to light it.

"What you want to see him about?" he said.

This would be Shane, the other deputy U.S. marshal. Part of Hewitt's practice was to make a few enemies in a new town, along with a few friends. It was time now to display a little calculated brutality.

"Sit up, damn your hog's soul, and say 'sir' when I condescend to speak to you," he said.

He leaned over the desk and knocked the Panama hat flying. He swiped downward with the ends of his fingers, giving a snap to his wrist at the right moment. He felt his fingernails rake the deputy's plump cheeks a smart, cutting blow.

Shane shrieked with surprise and pain. He slid backward, chair and all, clutching his smarting cheek with his left hand and fumbling at a drawer in the desk with his right. Hewitt tipped his .45 into his hand and shoved it across the desk.

"Take a look at that, Shane. Looks as big as a covered wagon bridge, doesn't it? And it's aimed right at your miserable heart," he said softly.

Fatty changed his mind about trying to get a gun out of the drawer. His pale greenish eyes came up to meet Hewitt's. "You're assaulting a federal officer, you know," he said. "You could go to the pen for this."

"You wouldn't make a pimple on a federal officer's butt," said Hewitt. "When I come into a public office, I expect civility. One more time—when do you expect Mr. Stambaugh?"

A long silence. Fatty had nerve, no question about that. He looked Hewitt over frowningly.

"By God, you must be Hewitt!" he shouted.

"Yes, and you must be Shane."

"Pat Shane. Oh hell, I sure am sorry about this, Mr. Hewitt!" Shane leaped up and offered his hand. "I always was an admirer of your'n. I never seen a detective before, and they say you're the best in the world. I thought you was another damn quarrelsome cowboy, wanting to try our prisoner for us. Say, will you show me that trick with your fingernails? It hurts so bad it blinds you, and yet it don't do a man no real damage, does it?"

"You can take a man's eye out, if that's what you want to do. Or you can merely teach him a lesson."

Shane grinned. "Like you done me. You set down here, Mr. Hewitt."

"Why, thank you, Mr. Shane." It was impossible to dislike Shane. He reminded Hewitt of a half-grown mastiff pup, most dangerous when he played.

"My friends call me 'Pat.' Anybody ever call you 'Jeff'? It sure would be an honor to me, if we could get right down to first names."

"Bet your life we can, Pat."

Hewitt took the chair. Shane sat on a corner of the desk and gave Hewitt a rapid summation of his entire life. His daddy had raised hogs in Tennessee. Last fall, his older sister's husband had got elected to Congress, and all he asked of the President was a good job for Pat. God-dang hogs wasn't paying too good and he didn't like taking care of hogs nohow, so here he was Deputy United States Marshal Patrick Shane!

Hewitt got him back to the subject eventually. "I came as soon as I got Mr. Stambaugh's letter. What's the big problem you have here?"

"Whoo-ee! It ain't one, Jeff—it's a whole gang of them. Main thing is, we ain't got no judge here. The sheriff they had, he up and took a quarry job, because he needed the money. He got killed in a cave-in, and there wasn't no witnesses. Law said there had to be an inquest.

"The county judge was going to hold one, so he called a lot of the quarrymen to testify, and they must've feared they was going to be held to blame. There was a riot that just about wrecked this courthouse, and the judge fired off a letter to the President and caught the next train out of town.

"The President, he sent in a federal judge, and this judge brought Lee Stambaugh with him. He put Lee under a court order to maintain the peace, and then *he* left town. Lee asked for help, and I was all that was sent in. Just me!

"Before any court will sit here again, or before they can elect a sheriff, Lee has got to satisfy this federal judge that there is law and order here. Which won't be easy.

"Then there's this murder. It happened just before the judge and Lee got here. The victim, a little girl, was already buried. The prisoner was already in custody. No death certificate, no inquest, no grand jury indictment—nothing! They just buried the girl and throwed this feller's hind end in jail. How that judge did sputter about that!"

Someone knocked on the door of the little office, and then the door opened. "Anyone at home?" a voice said.

Pat Shane threw up his hands in despair. "You!" he said. "Goddam it, haven't we got troubles enough? I was just telling Mr. Hewitt, the famous detective, about all the problems we've got here. I was saving you for some other time, when we're both stronger."

CHAPTER FOUR

The man in the door was one of the most handsome Hewitt had ever seen. At least six foot three, broad of shoulder but slim, rangy, lithe as a puma. Not yet forty, with a tumble of longish, golden hair and blue eyes. Smooth-shaven face, with the lost-lamb look you saw on some missionaries. He wore black serge pants tucked into flat-heeled eastern boots, and a black satin shirt with big pearl buttons.

If ever a man had gone out of his way to advertise himself as a tenderfoot, this was it. The very sight of him seemed to infuriate Pat Shane, but the newcomer remained unaware of Shane's fury.

"I'll have to apologize for being late, Pat, but I just couldn't help it. Shall I go on in?" he said.

"Why ask me, goddam it?" Shane choked. "I'm against this. If Lee says it's all right, then it's all right. But don't ask me!"

The stranger smiled. "I thought we had agreed to disagree on that, and be friends. You're in charge. If you say to get out of here, of course I'll do it."

Shane turned to Hewitt. "Who in the hell in his right mind would carry presents of food—good, home-cooked food by God!—to a child-killing rape murderer that's going to hang?" Shane looked back at the stranger. "And he *is* going to hang, ain't he?" he said, thickly. "Answer me that, Adrian. *Ain't* he going to hang?"

"Oh, I'm sure he is."

"Then what the hell do you care what he eats?"

"If I'm ever at the bottomless pit of despair, I hope someone will show me just a little kindness at the end. Which of us can be sure we won't end the same way? Just a little kindness, Pat—that's all. What does it cost us?"

"Mr. Hewitt, meet Adrian Johnco," Shane said. "Adrian, this is Mr. Jefferson Hewitt. You know who he is. But don't preach kindness to me! Tell that to the son of a bitch that murdered Loretta Patterson."

Johnco carried a basket covered by a white cloth and a pot with a lid on it. He put the pot on the desk to shake hands with Hewitt. He smiled a dreamy and rather shy smile, and his handclasp was a gentle one, swiftly disengaged.

"Welcome to Kaylee's Ford, Mr. Hewitt. This was a good town, and can be again."

"I am sure of that," Hewitt said.

Shane lifted a corner of the cloth that covered the basket. "What you feeding this animal today, Adrian?"

"Boiled beef, beets and onions with a sour cream dressing, deviled eggs—and in the pot, barley soup."

Shane appealed again to Hewitt. "His wife is the best cook in South Dakota, and he brings the leftovers here to feed the prisoner. The son of a bitch eats better than I do! He ought to be sentenced to eat the rest of his life at Mrs. Stillman's boarding house, like I have to."

Johnco smiled. "I'm afraid the Constitution would forbid that, as cruel and unusual punishment."

Shane had to grin. "Go on, be kind to him, Adrian! But it's Lee that's responsible, not me."

Johnco thanked him, nodded to Hewitt, and went down the corridor with his basket and pot. Shane closed the door. "What do you think of that, Jeff?"

"A missionary?" said Hewitt.

"No. He gets a check from somewhere back east, and he teaches a little music, and he paints oil pictures, the

purtiest goddam pictures you ever seen! He's a free-lance
doctor, too, and Doc Tabery says he's a damn good one.
Came here for his health, he says, and peace of mind."

"What's his interest in the prisoner?"

"Just that nobody else cares about him. Can you beat
that? If I was in charge here, that prisoner would've been
took care of long ago."

"Lynch law is a bad thing, Pat."

"So is rape murder of twelve-year-old girls!"

Hewitt said, "And two wrongs never make a right. We
could go on like this forever, only I no longer have the patience. I can tell you've never seen a lynching.

"Well, I have! Next, you'll say it would be hard for you
to fire on decent people, just to save your prisoner a hanging. To which I reply that by the time people have worked
themselves up to the point of a lynching, there are no decent ones left in the crowd.

"If it happens, Pat, watch their faces *as* it happens.
Listen to their voices. See them change before your very
eyes, from human beings to something less than human.
There's only one way to make them human again."

"What's that?"

"Shoot first, shoot straight, and shoot to kill. Let them
see what a dead body really looks like! Never forget this—
there are no human beings in a lynch mob! Unless you
can get that through your head, you'll never amount to a
hill of beans as a peace officer."

Shane scowled with concentration, with the effort of
learning. "If you say so, Jeff," he said, nodding. "I wish Lee
would try to teach me things like that. With Lee, though,
it's just do this, do that, and if you do it wrong, you're just
too ignorant to bother with."

Hewitt smiled and said, "I know, and yet that's how you
learn, Pat. It's how I learned what little I know. I wish he'd

get back, though. I've got to find a place to stay, and I'd like to have a bath, and change clothes."

"Lee is planning on you living here, with him. He bunks in the bullpen cell, so there's somebody on duty here, twenty-four hours a day."

"That suits me. I'll go get my suitcase—"

"Let me get it. Where is it?"

Shane was anxious to please. Hewitt told him about leaving his suitcase in the restaurant, and Shane said, "All right, I'll try to ransom it. But if it's leather, she's already got it cut up to make soup out of. I'll light the fire before I go, and—look here, Jeff, what we've got, right here in the courthouse!"

He opened a door in the rear of the little office, and showed Hewitt a stone-floored bath house, with a big, wood-burning water heater. He touched off the fire, and bustled out, saying, "Is your horse out back? I'll put him up in the barn, and give him a bait of grain. See that no-body steals our prisoner until I get back."

I like that fellow, Hewitt decided, and I've seen many a worse policeman. . . . He had a hunch that Stambaugh and Shane did not get along, a circumstance that would not make the job here any easier.

He went into the big bullpen cell, and as he crossed the corridor, he noticed Johnco standing at the other end of it. His voice was a soft murmur that apparently was not having any effect on the prisoner, because he still had his basket and pot in his hands.

The bullpen was an attractive, bachelor bedroom; Hewitt had paid good money for many a worse, and not just in hotels in the West, either. Besides the two bunks there was a big chest of drawers, a willow rocking chair covered with a brindle cowhide, and a shaving stand with a basin on it, and a mirror on the wall above it.

When he saw that mirror, Hewitt felt completely at

home. It hung on the wooden sheathing that covered the corridor bars, and unless he was badly mistaken—

He was not. He took the mirror down silently, and put it on the bunk. Behind it was a big knot, which he easily removed by working it with his thumbnail. And here he had a peephole from which he could see a good part of the corridor, and most of the rearmost of the two cells.

He could see Adrian Johnco only by leaning sidewise, but he could hear him clearly, despite the low, even tenor of his voice: "Don't reject friendship, Emil. So long as one human being is still your friend, life is neither hopeless nor useless. No matter what you have done, you're still a man, just as I am. Eat, man!"

The prisoner ignored him. He shuffled, rather than paced, back and forth across his cell. Hewitt studied him carefully.

The prisoner was a typical quarryman, a mass of muscle, about Hewitt's own height but weighing at least seventy pounds more. All he wore was a pair of old Levi's that had been cut off at the knees. His body was hairy. His uncut hair and beard, all the same saddle-leather color, were stiff and straight.

A big, shambling gorilla of a man, he seemed ready to drop from sheer exhaustion. Yet he kept shuffling, shuffling, shuffling on his big bare feet—two long steps and then a short one to the north, a pivot on the right foot, and two long ones and a short south.

It was hard to make out his face, between the dim light and all that beard, especially since he never did look up. He held his fists at his side, at the ready, and pumped his massive arms as he walked.

"Emil!" Johnco said, sharply. "I'm tired of this. Bring your cup here and have some soup."

The prisoner snatched up a tincup with no handle, from

someplace. He took it to the cell door and held it through the bars.

"Now, drink that, do you hear me? No, wait, man—there's more. Now," Johnco said, "put these other things on your bunk. You may not want them now, but you will later. I must go now, Emil, but I'll see you tomorrow."

When the prisoner carried the food over to his bunk, Hewitt got his first good look at his face. It was the face of something subhuman, brutal, and stupid—and yet so full of reeking sadness that Hewitt felt it like a blow from one of those massive fists. Thoughtfully, he replaced the knot, and then the mirror. When a man was so low he could not even kill himself—when he could not carry out his own sentence of death upon himself—he was indeed beyond all hope.

Pat Shane, returning with Hewitt's suitcase, met the departing Johnco in the empty front office.

"How did you and your friend enjoy your tea party, Adrian? He like his little goodies, did he?"

"He would only drink the soup. I left the other things with him."

"For me to get your goddam dishes back."

"He has never given you a problem there, Pat. Be fair! He always sets the dishes out in the corridor. Why do you bother to hate a man as close to the grave as him?"

"It's the principle of the thing with me."

"Poppycock! What does a little compassion cost you?"

"If I's running this jail, I'd give him a ten-foot start and compassion him right in the butt with some buckshot, that's what I'd do."

Johnco chuckled as he departed. For all the hard talk between them, he and Shane were friends. Shane came into the big cell carrying the suitcase. "This sure is a beauty, Jeff," he said, putting it on one of the bunks. "There's one here in town just like it that I sure wish I could own. I purely love good leather."

"That's a good one," Hewitt acknowledged.

"Mind telling me what it cost you? This fella wants ten dollars for the one he's got, just like new."

"That one was a gift from a grateful client." Hewitt smiled, remembering that this client had bought the matching case, in expectation of leaving town with him. It had not been easy to talk her out of it. "Ten dollars would be a fair price, Pat."

"I ain't been paid yet. Your bath water's hot, if you're ready."

"I'm ready."

The man who emerged from the bathroom an hour later was not the frowzy saddle bum who had ridden Rowdy into town this morning. He had straightened out his expensive hat, creasing it in the cavalry style. He wore a tailored frock coat, a white shirt, and a black bow tie. His black serge trousers were tucked into boots that had cost him fifty dollars in Chihuahua. His gold watch chain, hand-made by Yaqui Indians near Bacatete, Sonora, had been another gift from a grateful client.

And I would have taken her with me, he recalled. What a woman! The trouble with Mexican women, like all women, was that the old kiss-we-and-part business just wasn't true. The ones worth having parted without the kiss—if, that is, they already had husbands.

A man sat at the desk in the little office, a lean, smooth-shaven, hard-faced, cold-eyed man about an inch shorter than Hewitt. His prematurely gray hair had been clipped short. He wore the clothes of a working man—blue Levi's and a blue shirt—but cleaned and pressed like a gentleman's suit. I am what I am, his presence seemed to say, and you may suit yourself about liking me. . . .

"You make yourself right at home, Mr. Hewitt," he said,

looking Hewitt over coldly. "You and Shane are already on
first names, I note."

"Kindred spirits, I suppose. How are you, Mr. Stambaugh?" Hewitt said, offering his hand.

"A little upset, that's how," Stambaugh said, rising to
shake hands.

"About what?"

"You ride into town looking like a vagabond, you gumshoe around, asking questions and looking things over, as
though you thought I wouldn't hear about it."

"I didn't care if you did hear about it."

"Why not come straight to me?"

Robert E. Lee Stambaugh made it *so* easy to dislike him!
Only a bumptious lad like Shane would ever use his first
name freely. Hewitt said:

"Mr. Stambaugh, you hollered for help. I came. You
know that I work in my own way, or not at all. What did
you expect me to do, bring you flowers?"

Stambaugh smiled frostily. "I see your point of view. Sit
down and tell me what you think."

"I can tell you that standing up. I think you're going to
have a lynching party here."

"The cowboys or quarrymen?"

"Either."

"It won't be the quarrymen, Mr. Hewitt. They get off
the sidewalk when they see me coming. Five or six together
haven't the courage to face me."

"But how about two or three hundred of them? They'll
take this courthouse to pieces with their bare hands."

Stambaugh frowned. "Maybe. I think not, but I didn't
ask you here to agree with me. What else?"

"I think the best way to prevent a lynch riot is to assert
your authority now. The quarrymen have made the streets
unsafe for decent women. That's bad police work."

"I know that. If I had fifty patrolmen, maybe I could do something about it."

"Fifty wouldn't begin to do the job, if it's a question of numbers. Why do you let the quarry haul their rock through town? Make them move that wagon road—teach them, management and men both, that they have to get along with this town!"

Stambaugh said, "Have you ever done business with one of these aristocrats with a hyphenated name? Take the name of Edwin W. Newhart-Poulton, for instance."

Hewitt could not help laughing. "I know what you mean. Is Mr. Newhart-Poulton the quarry manager?"

"And majority owner. I'm not easy to bluff, Mr. Hewitt, and yet he walked off in the middle of a sentence, hyphen and all, and just ignored me. I've got connections in Washington, or I wouldn't have this job. I let him get away with it, because I know he has better connections. Suppose I just walk off the job—what do you think would happen, then?"

"Your prisoner would be lynched." Stambaugh nodded, and Hewitt went on: "There are ways of handling men like your Mr. Newhart-Poulton. I think I have met him. Tall, ugly, red-faced tenderfoot with a British accent?"

"That's the man."

"Suppose I try handling him?"

"Suit yourself. Anything you can—"

Both men dropped to the floor, as a sound no one could mistake, shrieked through the building. It was a bullet, a big one driven by a big powder charge. Stambaugh was the first to regain his poise. He stood up, grinning ruefully.

"Nothing to fear, Mr. Hewitt. Somebody shoots through the little window of the empty cell, between us and my prisoner. It's just one of the things that make this job interesting. It happens almost every morning."

"And there's nothing you can do about it?"

"I know where he's shooting from. There's only one place where he can be shooting over the roofs of those buildings across the street. I've been so damned alone!" Stambaugh pounded the desk lightly with his fist. "Pat Shane is a good errand boy, that's all. I need someone with judgment to carry part of the load."

"Mr. Stambaugh, detective work is just logic, patience, and hard work."

"And experience. Don't forget experience!"

Both men flinched, as another bullet shrieked through the cell next door. Hewitt stepped out into the corridor. The window of the cell was surely almost at the level of the sloping ground outside, but it was high up in the cell. The slug had ripped through the wood sheathing that covered the bars on the other side of the corridor, spending itself in the big room where Hewitt would bunk with Stambaugh.

"This is one of the things we're going to have to settle fast, Mr. Stambaugh," Hewitt said, returning to the office. "As long as they can twist your tail by firing into your jail, your authority is pretty shaky. You know that."

Stambaugh smiled without amusement. "Yes, I do. You whack Mr. Edwin W. Newhart-Poulton across the knuckles, and teach *him* about our authority, and maybe we can fall on some of these lesser miscreants, then."

"I'll rough him up in my own way. And I'll bet we move that road."

"That will make a big difference. Let the ladies of the town see we've got control, especially those who buy in Mrs. Johnco's store, and—"

"*Whose* store?" Hewitt cried.

"Mrs. Johnco. Have you met her?"

"In a way. I never heard her name."

"Her first name is Merle." Stambaugh squinted at him. "They make a handsome couple, don't they?"

"And a slightly puzzling one. Who are they?"

"He's supposed to have had the consumption. They've been here about a year. She's well-liked by the ladies, although she doesn't neighbor with them much. Johnco is—well, you know painters and musicians! He doesn't go out of his way to make friends."

"Except your prisoner. Tell me about him."

Stambaugh told him. The prisoner's name sounded like "Cheer-in." It was spelled "Tcherin," which sounded Russian to Hewitt. No, said Stambaugh—it was German. Emil Tcherin had only a little English, but he stammered so badly that even his German-speaking friends had trouble understanding him. His nickname, as a consequence, was "Baa Baa," even among the German quarrymen.

"I had Dr. Tabery examine him. He says there's no—" Stambaugh pawed through some papers on his desk, and came up with a notation of the word he wanted. "This is what he called it—ankyloglossia. It means tongue-tie. He just gets excited when he tries to talk, and the harder he tries, the worse he does."

Tcherin was a chronic drunkard. He had not had a drink in the six weeks he had been in jail, nor drawn a sober breath in the week before that. Stambaugh had given up trying to question a man who could only wave his arms and answer, "Baa—baa—baa—baa—baa!"

Stambaugh slouched at the desk, playing a nervous tattoo on it with his knuckles. "Suppose we could get a judge with guts enough to come in here and try him—how can a man defend himself when he can't even talk? A trial would be just another kind of lynching, Mr. Hewitt."

This man Stambaugh was by no means a run-of-the-mill political policeman. He learned about things like "ankyloglossia," and he resented the enigma the law failed to solve when a man accused of a hanging crime could defend himself only by saying "Baa."

"You do have your problems," Hewitt said.

Stambaugh glowered up at him. "You haven't heard my worst one," he said.

"What's that?"

"My prisoner isn't guilty."

CHAPTER FIVE

Somehow, Hewitt was not surprised. "Can you prove that?" he said.

"If I could, I wouldn't bother you."

Another rifle bullet shrieked through the cell next door. Hewitt felt his temper slipping. He held it in carefully.

"Eventually," he said, "that would get on my nerves."

Stambaugh nodded. "Yes. It has on mine."

"So I'm to prove your prisoner's innocence. How?"

"Why, the usual way. By proving someone else's guilt. My best estimate is that you've got close to one thousand suspects—all the quarrymen, all the cattlemen and cowboys, all the drifters that blow through a town like this, at this time of year.

"Mr. Hewitt, I've seen enough of miserable, sad, sinful humanity in my time to know a child-killer when I see one. I'm sure you have, too. The victim here was a nice twelve-year-old girl. It takes a certain kind of animal to commit that crime.

"As sure as God gave me a brain to think with, Emil Tcherin is not that kind! An animal, yes. A draft animal, an ox, one of those tame elephants that pile logs for the natives in India. But I've had him underfoot here for six weeks, and *I tell you he did not kill that little girl!*"

"Maybe you had better give me the whole story," Hewitt said.

"Let's go into the bullpen, where it's comfortable, and I'll put a pot of coffee on. I'll tell you about this crime, and then I've got a peephole where you can study my prisoner. I want you—"

"I've already found your peephole. You don't have to set the stage, Mr. Stambaugh. Let's get comfortable, as you say, and then don't be afraid to talk to me in grown-up terms."

Red-faced, Stambaugh stood up and stalked through the door and across the corridor to the bullpen. Another rifle bullet howled through the jail, but he did not show nerves. "Come on, Mr. Hewitt. He spaces his shots out, so you're perfectly safe," he said.

Loretta Patterson was only twelve, but she was a big girl with the mature figure of a grown woman. She was the fifth and youngest child of Nathan and Roma Patterson, and their only daughter. The oldest son was studying for the ministry in the winter, but was at home for the summer, working in the quarry. The next son was in California, teaching school. The two younger sons, seventeen and fourteen, helped their parents at home.

Nate Patterson ran a store, patronized mostly by reservation Indians, almost a mile north of town. He was also the town's undertaker. He did his embalming in Dr. Tabery's surgery, but kept a hearse and a white team at home. He also traded a few horses and cattle.

Roma, his wife, was an expert telegrapher who "worked the extra board" for the railroad, filling temporary vacancies anywhere on the division. She hoped someday to get the permanent job at Kaylee's Ford.

The Pattersons had some thirty acres, mostly pasture, under fence. Here they kept the family buggy horse, the hearse team, and the livestock he traded. There was a shallow canyon or draw through the property, leading up to a hilltop above the quarry. From that hilltop, the quarry, the tents where the quarrymen lived, the Patterson place, and most of the town of Kaylee's Ford was visible.

Loretta had been forbidden to climb the hill since the coming of the quarry. There was an old trail up to it, cut originally by Indians picking blackberries, long before the coming of the white man. Larger trees had long ago been cut, but there were a few runty ones left on the slope. One was known as "Loretta's Tree," because her father had once put a swing for her on one of its limbs.

The girl was last seen by Julius "Muley" Skintle, an old Pony Express rider who now worked in the livery barn. He went to the Patterson place to make a payment on the bill for his late wife's funeral. He deposed that he had met Nate Patterson on the road. Nate was going to town to get a horse shod and mail some letters.

"Loretta's to home. Pay her. I'm in a hurry, Muley," he said.

Muley rode on and tied his saddle mule in front of the house. Loretta heard him and came out, and he gave her his three-dollar payment. "I'll go put it in the book and write you out a receipt," she said.

"Oh shoot, I don't need no receipt!" he said.

"Papa says I've got to give a receipt, and doggone it, do you want to get me into trouble?"

"All right, all right, all right!"

He sat on the porch and fanned himself with his hat. In a few moments Loretta came out with his receipt, written in her clear, schoolgirl hand. Muley thanked her and rode away. He remembered looking back and seeing her standing in the door, with one of her bare feet flat against it, looking off dreamily at nothing.

Roma and the youngest boy, Clancy, had gone to the Indian reservation early that morning. Roma had given some families there a sow with pigs at side, and three hens with chicks. She had been teaching some of the younger

Indians how to raise pigs and chickens. They got home about five o'clock in the afternoon. Loretta had been told to pick some green beans and get them ready, and if they were not back by four, to put them on the stove.

The green beans were in a pot of water, but had not been put on to cook. There was no sign of Loretta. Roma was not particularly alarmed, knowing that the girl was at that nitwit stage, neither child nor woman. "Anyone who wants to be that young again," Roma said, "just doesn't remember what a miserable time it is. No, sir, I'll take middle-aged peace of mind any old day."

("Wait a minute!" Hewitt said. "A big, precociously developed girl, but a child in mind. Exactly the type to attract a madman, am I right?" Stambaugh nodded and frowned and asked Hewitt not to interrupt him again.)

Robert, the oldest boy, got home from the quarry at six-thirty. He was the one who first became alarmed about Loretta. "Forget supper, Mama, and let's find her," he said. "You and the boys look everywhere here. Clancy, be sure to look under the house, and even in the mangers in the old barn. I'll go into town for help. I don't like this at all."

There was no court, no sheriff. Robert found eleven men and big boys who were willing to help. One was Mr. Edwin W. Newhart-Poulton, who was exercising his little gray saddle mare.

"I say, damn it, we're only a handful and this may be a big job," Newhart-Poulton exclaimed. "Two of you come with me, and I'll stir out a few of my men—those who slightly resemble human beings. The others are capable of anything. I am very fearful, gentlemen—very!"

It solved a problem for the townsmen. They had thought of the quarrymen first, but had not known how to handle the problem. Newhart-Poulton simply ordered the men to leave their mess and go back to their tents and turn their cots over. They looked at him with murder in their eyes as they shook out their blankets, but they obeyed.

He found several bottles of liquor and fired their owners on the spot. But there was no sign of the girl. "I've seen Indians up there on the hill, coming from that place where the undertaker lives," Newhart-Poulton said, pointing.

"The Patterson place. That's where the girl we're looking for lives," someone said.

"I suggest we search there. I'll bring some of my rock heads." He turned and waved to a group of quarrymen, who would have killed any local man who called them rock heads. "You rock heads, come give us a hand! You can eat later," he said.

They followed. They crested the hill, climbed over Nate Patterson's barbed-wire fence. "Spread out now, men, and investigate anything large enough to conceal a human being. Look sharp, now!"

Not twenty yards away, they found Emil Tcherin asleep in the trail. His quart bottle was almost empty. He slept on his side, cuddling the bottle in the crook of his arm. Newhart-Poulton tore a sheet from his notebook, and printed on it, YOU ARE FIRED. He tucked it into Tcherin's pocket.

"Let's go, men. Look sharp!"

Ninety paces down the trail, under the tree known as "Loretta's Tree," they found her body. Newhart-Poulton described it in a written report, which Stambaugh showed to Hewitt:

"There was a little grass under the tree. The body was cold. It was dressed only in a faded brown dress, which had been pulled down to cover her nakedness. Nearby lay her knickers, a muslin undershirt, and a large bib apron. The sandy soil in which the grass grew displayed signs of a struggle.

"The only visible blood was on the girl's nostrils. Obviously, she had been hit in the nose, violently, before death. There were black-and-blue marks on her throat. We made no other examination of the body, since it would serve no useful purpose, we not being medical experts.

"We took Emil Tcherin into custody, carried him to the quarry, and hauled him into town in a wagon. We turned him over to certain residents of the town, who had formed an *ad hoc* committee to take charge of the jail and assume responsibility for prisoners.

"I had left two townsmen guarding the body. I requested Dr. Isaac Tabery, the local practitioner, to take charge of it and make whatever investigation might, in his best judgment, be required under the law. I wired the Attorneys-General of the state and the United States and requested that appropriate authority be notified to assume responsibility in the entire matter.

"No further comment by the undersigned appears to be necessary. Dr. Tabery's report speaks for itself. If I may be permitted a personal opinion, however, I wish I could express the enormous rage I feel that blundering frontier justice, so-called, will probably permit the horrible sacrifice of this lovely child to go unavenged."

Hewitt listened with only half his mind. The other half struggled with the enigma of Stambaugh himself. Back in Colorado, he had talked in a drawl that Hewitt, a student of accents, had identified with the hill country of West Virginia. He still had part of that accent—but not much, not much. And he talked with an excellent choice of words, like the educated man he obviously was not.

"I was in Arizona Territory when they wired me to come here and take charge," Stambaugh said. "They never did catch up with me, to tell me about the murder and about the telegrams old Double-Name had fired in. No, I had to

get off the train here and walk into it blindly. The deeper
I got into it, the blinder I became. I remembered your
promise, Mr. Hewitt, and for this dead girl's sake, had no
hesitancy about calling you."

Hewitt nodded. He remained silent for some time.
Then, "There's one possibility, Mr. Stambaugh," he said.

"What's that?"

"Cases occur where these big, precocious girls are not so
innocent. They lead a man on, and whether they know
they're doing it or not, they're exciting his lust in the most
flagrant ways. When it's too late, they break the news that
they're mere children. The terrified man thinks he won't
be in any worse trouble if he kills them, and may even
escape altogether. So we have murder."

"I know that. I have investigated this girl, and so has
Dr. Tabery. We're not entirely imbecilic, Mr. Hewitt. We
agree that she was a decent, mannerly girl who was *not*
seduced. She was knocked out by several blows in the face
and violently assaulted."

"How do the Pattersons feel about Tcherin?"

"Well, how would you feel? Muley Skintle is the worst,
embittered propagandist in town, however. He's for hanging Tcherin, legally or otherwise. I've tried to—*damn
that yellow coward!*"

Another rifle bullet had come shrieking into the jail.
Hewitt saw it smash into a wooden box in the corner of
the big cell they were in, and he knew now why it was there.
It would at least help prevent ricochets.

He went to the shaving mirror, removed it and the knot
under it, and stood there for several minutes, watching
the prisoner in his cell across the dark corridor. Tcherin had
exhausted himself with his barefoot pacing. He sat on his
bunk, half asleep, only half alive it seemed to Hewitt, and
nibbled at one of the deviled eggs Adrian Johnco had
brought.

He was the embodiment of despair, a human creature past human pity or human hope, unable even to give voice to his woes, a Job mute even to God. But what struck Hewitt most forcibly was the sudden realization that he had already decided that Tcherin was innocent. This Stambaugh was a persuader.

He replaced the knot and the mirror. "I have to take your word that this big fellow is innocent. You have had time to study him—I haven't. But you don't give me much to work with, and I think you already know that if good, hard work would prove your case, I wouldn't be here."

Stambaugh said, "It takes more than work. It will take inspiration, luck, the stubbornness of a vain man who thinks he is too good to lose."

Hewitt made a face. "That's a touching vote of confidence, but I need more."

"I'll give you more. Listen!

"Newhart-Poulton picked up five candy jelly beans in the dirt beside the body. Two pink ones, one red one, one white one, one black one.

"When I got around to the clothing, I found a big, deep pocket in the bib apron the girl had been wearing. There were sixteen jelly beans in it—four pink, three red, two black, two green, two white, three yellow.

"The family doesn't know this—nobody but Dr. Tabery. He opened her stomach and found a lot of candy in it, these same jelly beans, he thinks.

"The Pattersons sell jelly beans. So does nearly every store in town. But not like these! The ones found near the body and in the apron pocket are bigger and the colors are brighter. I wonder if this suggests anything to you?"

"Of course it does. That she was tempted like a child, by someone who knew she was only a child, someone who slugged and raped her when he couldn't seduce her with jelly beans."

Stambaugh nodded vigorously. He said, "And in that cell yonder is a poor, tongue-tied rock head with nothing on his mind except whiskey. Meanwhile someone is whistling about town, his pockets full of jelly beans—oh, Christ! Who is his next victim, Mr. Hewitt?"

"May I see those jelly beans?"

Hewitt admired Stambaugh's ingenuity in hiding them. Should the jelly-bean murderer suspect they were here and come looking for them, he would have his work cut out for him. Stambaugh had opened a fresh box of .45 cartridges, and had removed the bottom ones, that stood points up. He had filled the bottom of the box with the jelly beans and then stood the other cartridges in on top of them, points down.

From the top, only the honeycomb pattern of the brass jackets was visible, and the box was in plain sight, with another box, on the stand beside Stambaugh's bunk.

"Take some, Mr. Hewitt. What colors do you want?"

"The brighter ones."

"The pink and the yellow are more distinctive, more unlike the pink and yellow ones sold most places. You can look, but you won't find any like them here."

"Then I won't even look."

Hewitt wrapped the two jelly beans carefully in paper, opened his shirt, and slipped the tiny package under one of the straps of his shoulder holster.

"That's a dirty gun, a dirty way to carry it," said Stambaugh. "That's one of the reasons I have never particularly liked private detectives."

Hewitt said, "I know how you feel, but I would rather live without minor ethical laws than die for them."

"We all must compromise. What'll you do now?"

"Find a place to eat."

"Mrs. Stillman has her bad days, but sometimes you

can eat well there. It's where I eat. But after you find a place to eat—what then?"

"Talk to the Pattersons, and Muley Skintle. And tomorrow, I think I'll spend the morning up where this sharpshooter fires from."

"You feel that's of first importance?"

"Mr. Stambaugh, any time anyone is firing that close to me, he merits my earliest and most painstaking attention. Granted that he needs a lot of luck to hit me—I still don't like to be shot at."

"Good enough. I'll take you there before daylight. I rather hoped, though, that I was going to see some first-class detective work."

"You are," said Hewitt. "A first-class detective always takes care of his own hide before he does anything else."

CHAPTER SIX

Hewitt came awake and sat up, aware that it was earlier than he liked. As a rule, he could make up his mind when he wanted to wake up before going to sleep, and he would awaken almost to the minute. It took him a moment to realize that it had been another series of dynamite shots at the quarry that had stirred him out at this hour.

He struck a match and looked at his watch: five past three. Then he heard other sounds—the shuffling and grunting and occasional discontented bawling of cattle on the move. A herd was being moved through the town, from south to north. Not a small herd, either, and strung out by the narrow streets of the town.

He found a cigar in the dark and lighted it. He sat there thinking about his interview with Muley Skintle and Nate Patterson yesterday. Now and then he heard a cowboy singsonging, "Hyo, hyo, hyo," to the herd.

He had been lucky to find Muley and Nate together, at Nate's store. He liked the looks of the Patterson place—nothing fancy, yet neat and orderly, the place of a man who took care of what he had. He tied Rowdy beside the saddle mule in front and went in.

The chubby little man sitting on the counter with his ankles crossed would be Nate Patterson. He was plainly but neatly dressed, a mild little man without distinction unless you counted the new look of deeply ingrown pain on his face. That would never entirely disappear.

Muley Skintle sat in a creaking old willow chair, a wiry,

runty little man with beady, black eyes half hidden in a
nest of curly, graying whiskers. It had taken a certain kind
of man to ride the Pony Express, and Muley had those
qualities. Nerve. An inborn readiness to fight. The gambler's instinct, tempered by animal will to survive.

It was Muley that Hewitt approached, saying, "They
tell me you used to ride the Pony Express."

"What if I did?" Muley said.

"I used to have a friend who had too. C. B. Bennion.
No name—just the initials."

"Bennion—why by hell, I haven't thought of him in
years! Where is old C.B. now?"

"Last I heard, he was living with his married son in
Weeping Water."

"That'd be Nebraska." Hewitt nodded and Muley went
on, "C.B. turned out to be a money-maker, I hear. Not
many of us was."

Hewitt offered his hand, and Muley took it. "My name
is Jefferson Hewitt," Hewitt said. "Maybe you have heard
of me."

"The detective," Muley said. He broke contact quickly.
"The feller that's going to help get that damn rock head
out of a murder trial."

"By finding out who did it, Mr. Skintle."

"We already know that."

"No. The case against that poor sot in jail is a weak one.
And my experience has been that the trouble with con-
victing a man on bad evidence is that the real criminal
goes free. In this case, it would mean that some other
man's daughter is no longer safe."

He heard Patterson make a small, breathy sound of pain,
and went on, "If Tcherin did it, I mean to find the evidence
that will hang him. But I have to tell you this, I feel in my
bones that he's innocent. I want to clear it with you two

because I think you, more than anyone else, will want to be sure we hang the right man."

Muley Skintle looked at Patterson and seemed to find no guidance there. He stared at Hewitt a long time. "You ever been in San Bernardino?" he said, suddenly.

"In California? Yes, about five years ago. I worked an arson-murder case, a warehouse fire."

"Only you wasn't called Hewitt then."

"No, I was Aaron B. London on that one. If you were there, you may remember that I got a confession and a conviction in three weeks. Of course, I had a run of luck."

"It wasn't all luck." Muley looked at Patterson. "Nate, I say give him a chance. If he says Tcherin is innercent, likely he is. I seen this feller take a case out there in California—why, it was as plain as daylight to everybody! Only, everybody was wrong."

"I don't want to be wrong," Patterson said. "When I think of that big bull rock head they got in jail, though, I want to kill him myself."

"Not a bull, Mr. Patterson. A big, dumb ox, a beast broken to the yoke. My expert opinion is that he didn't kill your daughter, but opinion isn't good enough. Let's be sure."

"I want to be sure too. But I wish we could get it over with. It just seems to go on and on and on."

Roma Patterson came in then—a handsome woman who looked younger than her years. She did not recoil with indignation when he identified himself, and she did not object to suspending judgment on Emil Tcherin.

"If he's not guilty, why should I wish him evil? All we want is to be sure that this can never happen to somebody else's child," she said.

Hewitt liked her immediately. He cautioned all three against making statements in Tcherin's favor anywhere. "If the hotheads think you have switched sides, it may tempt them to speed up the trouble. What we really want to do is stop the lynch talk and give me a chance to work."

"Won't be easy, with a full moon coming up," said Muley.

"What has that got to do with it?"

"Barkeeps in the Battlefield Saloon was talking about it just the other day. They sell nearly twice as much whiskey during a hot full moon, July or August, than they do at other times. They say every saloon does."

"I didn't know that. It's a useful thing to know."

"It'd be easy to get up a lynch party with a full moon shining, Mr. Hewitt."

Well, he had made friends there, and he had learned something about the hot full moon. He had also determined that the jelly beans that the Pattersons sold were unlike those found at the murder scene. He had not distrusted Lee Stambaugh's testimony on that point, but it was nice to be sure.

Lee Stambaugh slept deeply and quietly, something that Hewitt, a sometime snorer, envied. Hewitt made up his mind and began pulling on his pants. He was sure he could find the hilltop from which the sharpshooter fired without Stambaugh's help, and he was used to working alone. He was almost dressed when Stambaugh turned over and yawned noisily.

"Little early, Mr. Hewitt, isn't it?" he said.

"A bit. A herd of cattle just passed through."

Stambaugh sat up and reached for his clothing. "On the way to Montana. Should be around eighteen hundred head, and up to a dozen trail hands. I heard they were on the way and sent word that if they came through Kaylee's Ford, come through after dark."

"So as not to risk a collision between the herd and the rock wagons?"

"Yes."

"That's looking ahead."

"I'm not entirely stupid."

"Just surly."

Stambaugh struck a match to light a lamp, and Hewitt saw his stony smile. "That's right, just surly. We would both be better off with a cup of coffee. I'll show you a little jewel of a device I bought from an Englishman a few years ago."

From the bottom bureau drawer, he took a small stove that burned alcohol. He put a small coffee pot on it, and in a few minutes had coffee ready.

"A handy little housekeeping gadget, for the working bachelor," said Hewitt, who liked his coffee.

"The British abuse it by making tea with it."

"There speaks your narrow mind, Mr. Stambaugh. Tea is not bad at all."

"When you can't get coffee, that is."

They were more at ease today than they had been yesterday. Certainly Stambaugh had cracked no jokes yesterday.

"I think your prisoner is waking up," Hewitt said. "How about a cup for him?"

"You can try. He doesn't make friends, though."

Hewitt filled a tin cup and picked up the lamp. Tcherin was sitting on his bare plank bunk, his face in his hands. He was starting, in despair, another long day of despair.

"Have a cup of fresh coffee?" said Hewitt.

Tcherin shook his head angrily.

Hewitt said, "It will do you good. Get the hell up on your feet, like a man, and come get it. We're trying to be decent to you. Don't sit there feeling sorry for yourself!"

Tcherin got up and came to the bars. It was not easy to transfer the handle of the hot cup from Hewitt's hand to his, but somehow they managed it. Tcherin sipped it cautiously. His beady eyes darted up to meet Hewitt's once or twice, but fell quickly.

"Good stuff," Hewitt said.

"*Ja*, good stuff," said Tcherin.

"Want some more?" When the prisoner merely nodded eagerly, Hewitt said, "Speak up! You won't even talk to Mr. Johnco, man. When somebody is trying to be decent to you, the least you can do is speak to him."

"*Ja*, I like some more, please," Tcherin said.

Hewitt took the lamp and went for the coffee pot. Tcherin held his cup through the bars, and Hewitt filled it.

"Hits the spot," Hewitt said.

"*Ja*, hits the spot."

"You like a little sugar in it?"

"No, is fine, thanks."

"Take your time with it. Now, listen! Mr. Stambaugh and I are going to lay for this jaybird who has been shooting through the window here. You'll be all right until we get back. We'll have the courthouse in sight most of the time, and we'll be here before anything can happen to you."

Tcherin nodded, but he retreated visibly into his shell. Stambaugh locked the cellblock behind them, when they went out.

"That's an odd one," Stambaugh said, as they saddled their horses in the dark. "He talked to you, as plain as day. I've told him I'm on his side, but I never could get a word out of him."

"At least we know he can talk."

"If nobody's pushing him, maybe."

"There may be an idea in that, Mr. Stambaugh. Let me think about it."

Stambaugh led the way to the fork of the Y in the center of town, and then turned sharply up the other branch of it in the dark. Not a light gleamed in any of the houses, but the sounds of the quarry crew, waking up in their tents half a mile away, came clearly.

Stambaugh could not get Tcherin off his mind. "That poor, dumb animal! So damned grateful for a cup of coffee and a kind word. A good dog has more sense."

"I doubt it. I didn't get the feeling that he is a stupid man."

"Any man is stupid who breaks rock for a living."

Hewitt said thoughtfully, "Not if you have a problem expressing yourself. I remember one so-called tongue-tied witness. I got him to talk clearly, and at some length, by giving him tincture of opium. I wonder what Tcherin could tell us?"

"You do get around, don't you?"

"It's part of the job. You can usually find an answer to your problem if there's a fat fee riding on it."

"If money means that much to you."

"It does to me."

"You'll get no fee out of this, you know."

"No, and I'm not helping you because of your sunny disposition, either. You were useful to me once. You may be useful to me again. I pay my debts."

They had left the houses behind, but a narrow road still wound up the canyon. Stambaugh pulled up under a tree. "Better tie our horses here and go the rest of the way afoot," he said.

They tied their horses to the bottom branches of a tree, Stambaugh pulled a .30-30 carbine from its boot on the saddle, and they began walking. In a moment, Hewitt could see another house squarely across the end of the road ahead of them, half hidden among trees.

"We're not cutting through somebody's yard in the dark, surely," he said in a low voice.

"That's Johnco's place. He won't care. Probably won't even wake up." Stambaugh stopped and thought it over.

"You're right. He's not an early riser, but it is probably smart to wake him up."

"I would rather do that than have him shoot me."

Stambaugh grunted and walked up the path to the front door. It was a small house and very old, the battens warped and unpainted, and the split-log stoop half rotted away. Stambaugh rapped sharply on the door, and in a few moments, rapped again.

"Yes? Who is it, what do you want?" came Johnco's sleepy voice.

"Lee Stambaugh. Mr. Hewitt is with me," Stambaugh said, "and we want to cut across your property. Mr. Hewitt has some objection to being shot as a trespasser."

"I don't understand all this. Let me light a lamp and I'll be with you, Lee."

They heard a chain dropping inside, the door opened, and Adrian Johnco looked out at them. He had a blanket wrapped around him and was barefoot. "What in the world time is it?" he said, yawning and blinking.

"About four."

"What did you say you're doing?"

Stambaugh explained. "I should have let you know last night, save waking you at this hour."

Again Johnco yawned. "I'd ask you in for a cup of coffee, but my wife has been suffering with headaches, and I slept on the couch. I hope she hasn't waked up."

"We've had our coffee. Go back to sleep, Adrian."

"I'll do that. You have my hearty moral support, if that will comfort you."

They heard the heavy chain being locked again, as Stambaugh led the way through the trees. They climbed steeply for a few minutes. Now it was suddenly growing lighter and they could easily see their way.

They emerged on a bald hilltop—a double one, rather, perhaps three or four acres where the soil was too thin over the rock to support trees. They could see the town clearly now, at least the south end of it. The courthouse was in plain view, the two tiny cell windows barely visible above the roofs of the Battlefield Saloon and the ramshackle buildings beside it.

"This is the only place he could be shooting from," Stambaugh said. "You see how much chance there would be to corner him up here."

"He's a good shot, if he can hit those windows from here," Hewitt said thoughtfully.

"Better than I realized. One of these days, he'll see something to shoot at, and he'll hit it. We had better take cover where we can, Mr. Hewitt, and hope when he turns up, we've got him between us."

"Right! But what'll you bet he doesn't show up at all?"

"That's possible. He misses a day every now and then. Or do you know something I don't know?"

"You know everything I know, I assure you."

"But you're drawing some inferences that are still beyond me."

"I'm testing one. Let's get hidden."

Stambaugh squinted at him suspiciously, perhaps a little resentfully, but he made no comment. They took their positions a good hundred yards apart. Stambaugh, who had the carbine, went to the other side of the clearing and lay down in the brush.

Hewitt sat down under a tree, where he could see not only the courthouse, but part of the winding road that led to the Johncos' place. At eight fifty-five, he saw Mrs. Johnco walking rapidly toward town to open her store. She wore the black skirt she had worn yesterday, but today with a pale blue waist. Around her throat was a silk scarf of a slightly darker blue.

Even at this distance, she was an exciting woman to watch in motion. What a magnificent body, and what

gifted grace in her strong, swift walk! She was a woman
who could wear anything, be at home anywhere. On this
quiet, wooded path, she was all restrained passion and
beauty—in some millionaire's crowded ballroom, she would
have been the most vivid woman there.

He was sorry when she passed out of sight. A little later,
he heard Johnco come outside and call to the red squirrels.
They knew his call and came running to be fed. Hewitt
could hear them scolding Johnco, and Johnco scolding
them back.

They stayed at their posts until almost noon, and it was
Stambaugh who gave up first, and came walking through
the thin hilltop grass with his carbine. "I wish I knew why
you figured he would not be here today," he said, as Hewitt
stood up and joined him to walk down the hill.

"Nothing to it, Mr. Stambaugh. He surely knew of my
arrival in town. He made it clear how he felt about it, by
all yesterday's shooting. He would be a fool, though, to
imagine a professional detective wouldn't take steps."

"That's how you figure it, is it?"

"Yes."

"Mr. Hewitt, you're a liar."

It was said without heat, and Hewitt did not take of-
fense. When they reached the bottom of the hill, they saw
Johnco sitting on an old keg in the front yard, his back
to them. He was sketching something on a paper held on
a board on his knee.

Stambaugh shook his head: *Don't interrupt him!* When
they were untying their horses, he said, "I've heard you
never interrupt an artist at his work. I never met an artist
before, so it's hearsay to me. It's a talent I don't possess in
the slightest degree."

"I do some drawing and painting, but I can't call it art.
I know just enough about it to admire anyone who is
really good at it."

They mounted their bored and restless horses, and gave them their heads. They went back to the courthouse at a trot. Pat Shane was mopping out the entire sheriff's department, and had moved Tcherin into the adjoining cell until the floor of his own cell dried.

Stambaugh exploded. "You are trying to get that man killed! Do you think I want to lose a prisoner to a sharpshooting sniper? Put that man back where he belongs!"

"It's still wet in there, Lee, and—"

"Put him back! That's an order." Stambaugh went into the small office and closed the door.

Shane unlocked the cell and pointed. "Back home you go, you rock head! I ort to make you do the rest of this damn mopping."

Tcherin held out his hand for the mop. He tried to talk, and it did indeed come out, "Baa . . . baa . . . baa." Shane merely pointed again, and the big, hairy, barefoot man trotted back to his own cell and locked himself in.

On impulse, Hewitt went out to the stable and got Rowdy out again. He rode straight to the little sewing shop run by Mrs. Johnco. "Oh, hello, Mr. Hewitt," she said, when he came in. "I was just about to lock up and go home for luncheon. Is there something you want?"

"I wondered how your headache is, ma'am."

"It came back."

"Do you want me to try to ease it for you?"

Their eyes met, and he saw her color rise as she hesitated. He knew what her decision was going to be, and he was right.

"It would be so kind of you," she said, and began untying the blue scarf around her throat.

He came to the counter. She put her elbows on it, and rested her face in her hands. He touched the back of her neck delicately, seeking the cramped muscle that was pinching a nerve somewhere.

He found it at last, and traced it gently. "So you know who I am, ma'am," he said.

"Oh yes, everyone in town knew, soon after you arrived. My husband was much impressed by you."

"That's kind of him. I wish I could see some of his pictures, sometime. I fiddle at drawing and painting myself, in a petty way."

"He would be delighted to show them to you. No one here can discuss art intelligently with him."

"I'm sure I would fall somewhat short of real intelligence, ma'am, and surely nothing infuriates a real artist like the pretensions of a dabbler."

"I hardly think you could be a dabbler, Mr. Hewitt."

"Don't misunderstand me, Mrs. Johnco. I do my best, at whatever I do. I have a few modest gifts, but art is one of the most modest."

"What are those you rate higher?"

"This, ma'am. Now how is the headache?"

He took his hand away, and for a split second, she did not move. When she did look up, her expression took him by storm. Her face was flushed, her eyes bright. Her lips were parted.

He responded deliberately, holding her eyes with his as he leaned across the counter. For one or two heartbeats, she leaned closer to him. Her eyes half closed. The tip of her tongue came out to dampen her lips.

He sensed before she did, that she was going to catch herself in time. He took her hand from the counter and bowed over it, touching it lightly with his lips. She let him, and when she withdrew the hand, he did not try to hold it.

"No," she whispered, "you're not a dabbler."

"Then," he said, "we understand each other, don't we?"

"Yes," she said. "The headache is gone. Thank you so much for your kindness, Mr. Hewitt."

CHAPTER SEVEN

A cowboy crew, riding wearily in small, disjointed groups, crossed ahead of Hewitt as he reached the Y. He shook the picture of the woman out of his mind with an effort, and counted them. Sixteen weary trail hands, and another five or six out where they had bedded down the tired cattle.

He pulled in and let them pass. He fell in behind them, and saw them tie at the Battlefield when he crossed to the courthouse. He watered Rowdy and put him in the corral, still saddled.

Stambaugh was at his desk, reading a book. He closed it over a bookmark and put it in the bottom drawer of his desk when Hewitt came in.

"When do you eat?" Hewitt asked him.

"As soon as Pat gets back. I told him you and I would go together. He should be back soon."

"That trail crew just tied at the Battlefield."

Stambaugh nodded. "I've been expecting them. We have time to eat. We might even catch a nap. But I think we can count on some trouble from them."

"My feeling too. Why don't you go eat, and bring me back some sandwiches? I don't distrust Pat Shane's nerve, but he's inexperienced. I wish one of us could be here at all times."

"That makes sense."

No word waster, Stambaugh got up, reached for his hat, and went out. Hewitt waited until he heard the horse canter off, and then sat down and deliberately opened the drawer in Stambaugh's desk.

It was full of books. The top one was *The Six Best-beloved Tragedies of Shakespeare*. Hewitt opened the book and went through it: *Hamlet—Julius Caesar—Richard III—Romeo and Juliet—King Lear—Macbeth*. His bookmark was at the opening of Act IV: ii.

> Lady Macduff
> What had he done, to make him fly the land?
> Ross
> You must have patience, madam.
> Lady Macduff
> He had none:
> His flight was madness . . .

Hewitt looked at the bookmark, on which was written a list of words: incipient, sibilant, arkwright, chancery, incarnate, trapezoid. He looked through the other books: A frayed dictionary, an advanced speller, an advanced grammar, the *Collected Works of Lord Tennyson*.

He closed the drawer; he had Stambaugh's measure now. He could remember the same secret vice himself, like a drinker's thirst, the overpowering need of an ignoramus for knowledge. Knowledge! And the more a man got of it, the more possessive the addiction. So long as a man's knowledge was inferior to anyone else's—*anyone*—he was suspicious, stand-offish, cold.

So Mr. Robert E. Lee Stambaugh was a Virginia illiterate addicted now to the narcotic of words. Just as Hewitt had been a Missouri illiterate with the same excruciatingly possessive desire.

Shane, whistling noisily, put his horse up in the corral and came inside. "I wish the Battlefield would catch fire one of these days," he said blithely. "It's full of cowboys today. Bunch of trail hands headed for Montana. You're soft in the head if you want to go there anyway. Get a little liquor in you, and whoo-*ee!*"

"They'll bear watching," Hewitt agreed.

Shane pitched his hat at a nail, missed, and let the fine Panama fall to the floor. "I sure do like that suitcase of yours. Listen, will you do me a favor? Go with me to look at the one this fella has for sale."

"Not much advice I could give, Pat. If it's the twin of mine, it's a good one."

Pat wanted to talk about the suitcase, and he did so until Stambaugh came back, bringing sandwiches, pie, and two apples for Hewitt's lunch. Stambaugh got out the little British stove again and made coffee. He said then that he was going to get a nap and hoped Pat would lower his voice a little, and he urged Hewitt to do the same.

"I mean to," Hewitt said.

Stambaugh went into the bullpen cell, closing the door behind him. "He can make up his mind and drop off to sleep just like *that,*" Pat said, in a low voice, snapping his fingers.

"I envy him," said Hewitt.

It was hard for Shane to be quiet. He roamed the bottom floor of the courthouse restlessly. Some fifteen minutes passed, and then Shane came in from outside.

"An old codger coming up out of the brush from the back way, Jeff," he said. "He's up to no damn good, and I'm going to collar him if it wakes Lee up or not."

"Who is it?"

"Name of Earl Godfrey. He drives the stage and—"

"He's a friend of mine. If he's coming in the back way, it's for a reason. I'll go meet him."

"Dad-blamed if you don't make some queer friends," Shane grumbled.

He followed Hewitt to the door. There were no buildings in sight below the courthouse. It was Godfrey, and as he came out of the trees and brush at the bottom of the slope, he walked rapidly and furtively. Hewitt took note that he kept the courthouse between him and the Battlefield Saloon.

"Hello, Mr. Godfrey," Hewitt said. "Hot day for a stroll, I should think."

"Yes, and I ain't walked this fur in ten years," the stage driver said. "Like to talk to you a minute, just you and me."

"About the crowd at the Battlefield?"

Godfrey shot a suspicious glance at Shane. "Well, yes," he said hesitantly. "It's nothing to me what happens to that damn rock-head murderer. But I figgered you had a right to know they're working up to it."

"We thought that was possible, and I'm glad you felt like warning me, Mr. Godfrey."

"They can have Tcherin, but there's no use of you getting hurt, Mr. Hewitt."

"No, they can't have Tcherin. Somebody will get killed if they try it."

"If that's the way you feel—" Godfrey said.

Hewitt took him firmly by the shoulder. "Hold on, there! Even if I thought Tcherin was guilty as hell, I don't hand over a prisoner to a mob. And for your own, private information, this poor quarryman is innocent."

Godfrey's face reflected his doubts. Hewitt went on: "This used to be a good town, Mr. Godfrey. It's going through hell. It will never be fit to live in again if these trail hands are allowed to take this poor devil out and hang him just for sport. You live here. You ought to be on our side!"

It took time, but he brought an ally into the fight. Godfrey's old .44 was a good weapon in the right hands. He had only the six bullets in the cylinder, but that meant six more shots on their side.

The noise from the Battlefield increased steadily. Lee Stambaugh came out of the bullpen cell, wide awake and apparently perfectly calm. He stood listening to the racket from the saloon a moment.

"Pat, I think we ought to take us a couple of hostages," he said, yawning and stretching. "Let's go get us two more prisoners."

"Just drunks?" Pat said disgustedly. "Since when are you jailing drunks in this town?"

"Hostages, I said! If they take a notion to pull our jail down, I want a couple of their friends in here with us."

"It won't work, Mr. Stambaugh," Hewitt said.

"Why not?"

"You're assuming that these fellows are going to be thinking, if they decide to come in after this prisoner. That's the one thing they won't be doing. They'll be in a mood to kill women and children, if they have to, to get at their man."

Stambaugh hesitated. "Won't lose anything, anyway. Give me a chance to scold these rannies a little."

"Want me to go along too?"

"To arrest a couple of drunken trail hands? I hope you don't think I'm entirely helpless, Mr. Hewitt."

He went out, Shane hurrying after him. Soon the racket from the Battlefield rose sharply, and then died down except for the bray of Shane's raucous, carrying voice: "Do like Mr. Stambaugh says and no goddam sass! Get moving! And the rest of you, cut out this noise or I'll be back and choke it off, you hear?"

Hewitt could hear one of the women in the cribs above the Battlefield, shrieking obscenities after the two federal marshals. He could not help grinning at Godfrey, as the two crestfallen prisoners came reeling and stumbling into the jail. Shane opened the cell door for them.

"Get in there, you dogs! No—shut up—I don't want no

back talk! And no fighting, either. Remember one thing—no matter who loses the fights in our jail, we're the ones that win them."

The two new prisoners were somewhat the worse for wear. Apparently they had resisted arrest, and Stambaugh had let Shane overpower them at his pleasure. Shane clanged the door shut and handed the key to Stambaugh.

"Now will you go with me to look at that valise, Jeff?" he said. "It's going to be quiet for a while. I sure would like to have your advice."

Hewitt looked at Stambaugh, who smiled and said, "Go ahead. I think Earl and I can handle any emergency."

There were eight men and one woman milling in front of the Battlefield, when Hewitt and Shane went outside. They fled back into the saloon when they saw the two get their horses out. It could be taken for granted that calm would prevail for a while, at least.

Shane led the way to a small furniture store. The merchant got the suitcase down off a shelf, wiped off the dust, and opened it on the counter for them. "This is a beautiful piece of luggage, and like new," he said.

"See, it's the twin to your'n," Shane said, wistfully.

"Not quite like new," Hewitt said, pointing to a printed hotel sticker. "How much do you want for it?"

"Eight and a half. I didn't feel like haggling with the owner, and I'm entitled to a small profit."

"Is it worth it, Jeff?" Shane pleaded.

"I'm sure it is. Go ahead and buy it."

"Would you take fifty cents down, and hold it for me until my paycheck catches up with me?" Shane asked the merchant.

Hewitt took out his deerskin purse and found a ten-dollar gold piece. "You're Mr. Hewitt, the detective, aren't you?" the merchant said. "It's a pleasure to serve you. You're badly needed here. Let's make it eight dollars."

Hewitt thanked him and handed the suitcase to Shane. It was not hard to break away from Shane, who could think only of getting his beautiful new suitcase back to the courthouse to show to Stambaugh. Hewitt put Rowdy into a swift run, and in a few moments, tied before Nate Patterson's store.

He was in luck—Mrs. Patterson was on duty in the store. "I have a favor to ask you, ma'am, if it can be done without getting anyone in trouble," he said.

"Is it part of your investigation?"

"Yes, ma'am. It may be a very important part."

"I'll do anything I can."

"Is it possible for me to send telegrams from here without the agent knowing about it? I may want to do so from time to time."

"He would have to know about it eventually," she said. "I could hold the copies out of the files, and hold the money back too. You would have a month's time, about, but what about the replies?"

"I'm not worried about that at this time. The main thing is, I want this first one to go as soon as possible."

She called one of her sons to watch the store. "I'll have it on the wire in ten minutes."

"What if the agent is there, ma'am?"

"He'll have several telegrams piled up, hoping I'll come in and send them for him. And don't worry—he can't read half as fast as I can send."

The message was addressed to his partner, Conrad Meuse, Bankers' Bonding & Indemnity Company, Cheyenne, Wyoming. It said:

WHERE IS PEDISQUOD HOTEL URGENT PRIVATE

He helped her get her buggy out, and rode beside it until she turned off to go to the depot. He sat there a moment, listening in the hot, still air. There was still no resumption of the revelry at the Battlefield, but he was uneasy about tonight.

He rode to the quarry, where he had to be firm with Rowdy, to get him to enter the dark tunnels. Inside the hill was a honeycombed network of shafts and drifts, the "faces" where the men were working lighted by big coal-oil flares. He found the two deserters, Toby Parmenter and Mac MacAdams, working gloomily in the least-desirable tunnel face—the one deepest in the quarry, and farthest from the mess tent.

"How goes it, boys?" he said, dismounting.

Toby let his heavy, wedge-shaped sledge hammer fall, to study his blistered palms. "No way in the world you can load fifty tons a day!" he said. "You lied to us. We'd be better off working cows on somebody's spread at thirty a month and found."

"Only you haven't got a job working cows, and you do have jobs here. Hold my horse, and let me see if I can't show you a few tricks with a fourteen-pounder."

"*My* horse," Toby corrected him.

Hewitt took the hammer and went at it lazily. "Don't fight rock, boys. Note where it will break easiest, and then don't hit it—just let the hammer fall on it. A lick here—*ha!*—a lick there—*ha!*—another lick here—*ha!* And we have two rocks, where there was one before."

"You make it look so easy," said Mac.

"No, it's never easy, but every job has tricks."

"Where'd you learn it?" said Toby.

"In a federal prison. I won't say which one, but it was so hot, it makes this seem like a summer resort."

"What was you in for?"

"For the six weeks it took me to get the evidence to convict the prison administration on two counts of murder, twenty-two counts of various forms of financial chicanery, and one of felonious assault. Against me."

They heard the clink of horseshoes on the stone floor. Toby and Mac began to work furiously. In a moment, the arrogant man Hewitt now knew to be Mr. Edwin W. Newhart-Poulton rode into the dead-end tunnel on a handsome little gray mare.

"You're that detective chap," he said. "What are you doing here?"

"Looking for you," said Hewitt.

"You're supposed to be investigating the murder, I believe. I related everything I know in a written report. I can't help you further."

"No, but I can help you."

The quarry boss raised one eyebrow. "To do what?"

"You've got a long summer and fall ahead of you here. You have gone out of your way to make the people of Kaylee's Ford detest you. I'm sure you're aware of that."

Newhart-Poulton shrugged. "I'm sorry if people are unhappy. One can't have rock without quarries."

"Yes, but why run your wagons through town? Any other route would please the townspeople. Why go out of your way to offend everybody?"

Newhart-Poulton said impatiently, "That road was already in existence. It's the shortest route with the proper grades—downhill loaded, uphill empty. Did you expect me to build a new road?"

"Why not? Take the slope down Nate Patterson's hill. It's only a little longer, and you've still got the favorable grades."

"And I would have to buy right-of-way from Mr. Patterson. You're being ridiculous, Mr. Hewitt. How much do you want for your horse?"

"He isn't for sale. Let me persuade you that you haven't thought this road matter through," Hewitt said. "You dammed up a creek, and left a pond behind that fill to stagnate and breed mosquitoes to plague the town. No one has done anything about it yet, but how much trouble do you think it would be to dynamite that fill?"

"I don't take kindly to threats, so don't bother to make them."

"I'm not threatening. I'm just prophesying."

"May I try your horse? I may make you an offer you can't refuse."

"Try him, but don't count on owning him. Let me help you adjust the stirrups."

Hewitt held the gray mare when Newhart-Poulton rode off on Rowdy. Toby and Mac waited until they were sure the quarry boss was out of hearing.

Then Toby said: "What was that about dynamiting that fill? Who is going to do it?"

"Someone, eventually, I'm sure," Hewitt said. "How much could it cost? Ten dollars for dynamite, another ten for some experienced powder-monkey, and no more road, no more rock wagons, no more mosquitoes."

"Who would pay the twenty dollars, though?"

"Shame on you! I hope you boys aren't thinking about risking your liberty for a few dollars."

"Listen," Toby growled, "I can get into the powder-house, and we know how to handle dynamite. Do you know who wants that road blowed up?"

"You boys haven't thought this through," Hewitt said. "It would probably be worth—oh, maybe as much as fifty dollars—for a good job. One that would make it sure the road couldn't be repaired in a few days. That means a dozen shots, at least. A dozen chances to get caught—a dozen chances to blow your own heads off."

"I can set out two dozen, on half-hour fuses, and there's plenty of moonlight to work by. Do you mean that, Mr. Hewitt? Can we get fifty dollars for it?"

"I think so." Hewitt shook his head. "But I'm against it. It's illegal, it's risky, and it's a dirty trick against the man who pays your wages. I advise against it. I'm your friend, boys, and—"

Mac uttered an explosive vulgarity. They could hear Newhart-Poulton returning on Rowdy. Mac said, "You just find out if the job is worth fifty, and it's as good as done. We'll see you tonight sometime."

"I'll be at the jail. There's a bunch of cowboy trail hands thinking of breaking in and lynching the prisoner. It won't be safe there, boys."

"Ain't no bunch of cowboys going to make us no trouble," Toby said, picking up his hammer. "You just be there, *and don't you sell this bastard my horse!*"

"How much?" Newhart-Poulton said, pulling Rowdy up beside Hewitt.

Every man had his weakness, and horses were Newhart-Poulton's. He wanted Rowdy so badly, he had lost all judgment. He dismounted, and Hewitt shortened the stirrups again and swung into the saddle.

"Don't bother to make an offer, sir," he said. "You couldn't buy him for a million. A pompous ass who arrogantly offends a decent city, rather than move his damned, two-bit road, has no business owning a decent horse. Good afternoon, Mr. Newhart-Poulton."

CHAPTER EIGHT

Hewitt and Earl Godfrey went to supper at sundown, leaving Stambaugh and Shane at the jail. The atmosphere at Mrs. Stillman's boarding house was nervous and tense. Not one person mentioned the possibility of a lynching— all the proof that Hewitt needed that it was on everyone's mind.

A few of the people at the long table might have been for a lynching, he thought, although most would be against it. But all were vulnerable on one point. All wanted this protracted unpleasantness, which had spoiled their own town, ended one way or another.

There seemed to be twice or three times as many men in the Battlefield, and lounging in front of it, when they returned to the courthouse to relieve Stambaugh and Shane. Stambaugh confirmed this.

"Shingle mill and its logging crew west of town," he said. "They blew a cylinder head on their steam engine, and are shut down for a while."

"They could have picked a better time," said Hewitt.

Stambaugh nodded soberly. "Look, Pat and I will be as fast as we can. I'd advise you to think of your horse first, if they hit you while I'm gone. Turn him loose."

"You and Pat take him, and tie him somewhere else. Are your prisoners nervous?"

"Tcherin isn't. The two saddle bums are. It's good for their souls."

Shane, who did not own a horse, rode Rowdy when he

and Stambaugh went to dinner. Hewitt went into the jail. The two drunken cowboys—not so drunken, now—spoke to him as he passed them.

"Later." He went to Tcherin's cell, where the quarryman had resumed his pacing. "Are you afraid, Emil?"

Tcherin did not answer. Hewitt wondered if the man had even heard him. The calluses he had grown on his big, bare feet, in all these days and weeks of pacing, now made a clicking sound as he shuffled. Hewitt watched his chance and shot his arm between the bars.

He caught Tcherin, but lost his grip as the man turned. He caught some of the curly hair that grew so thickly on the arm, though, and the unexpected sting got through to Tcherin.

He whirled back, menacingly, lunging at the bars like a caged animal, but Hewitt had already withdrawn his arm.

"Emil, very soon we could have serious trouble here," he said, sharply. "Nobody's going to turn you over to them, understand? If it looks like they're going to get inside, we'll turn you loose and arm you. So quiet down! Don't lose your head. One of us will be here, before any of those drunks can—do you understand?"

From the next cell, one of the trail hands said, "He don't understand nothing. He's a goddam animal!"

"Shut up," Hewitt said.

"Who the hell you telling shut up? You lock a man up in your goddam jail with that raping animal—*ah-h-h-h!*"

There were two screams, really—first the familiar one of a rifle bullet, and then the terrified man's. For a moment, Hewitt thought he had been hit. My own nerves are jumping, he scolded himself. I didn't expect this, and I should have . . .

"Down, get down on the floor, back against the wall under the window," he shouted.

The two cowboys, now thoroughly sobered, flung them-

selves back. Earl Godfrey appeared in the office door at
the other end of the corridor. Hewitt motioned him back.

"He'll squeeze off another one or two. Don't take
chances! Just stay out of the way, and he can't hit anything."

"Let us out of here," one of the cowboys whimpered.
"Give a man a chance! You can't leave us in here to be
potshot."

"Who is it?" Godfrey wanted to know.

"Someone up on top of the bald hill east of town. He's
been having his fun for quite a while, Stambaugh tells me.
But one thing at a time. First we—"

It was as though he had expected the second slug, which
shrieked through the tiny window at this moment. He
could not help admiring the man's marksmanship. Even
with a bright moon, even with a steady rest on which to
lay the rifle, even with the daylight experience that had
made the target familiar, this was excellent shooting.

The two cowboys, crouching in the safest place in the
jail—against the stone wall below the window, where not
even a ricochet posed much danger—were begging to be
freed.

"I'll let one of you out," Hewitt said, "and I'll put the
other one in the cell with Tcherin. I'll let you decide between you who goes and who stays."

Neither wanted to stay and share a cell with the man
they had been planning to lynch. It seemed to Hewitt that
Tcherin was the calmest man in the building, and why not?
A rifle bullet might be a mercy to him.

The sharpshooter did not fire again. Stambaugh and
Shane returned, carrying double-barreled, twelve-gauge
shotguns and a big supply of shells, both birdshot and
buckshot. Hewitt felt better. A shotgun was the best riot
weapon of all.

Hewitt told him about the two rifle shots. Stambaugh

closed his eyes to think it over, then he said, "Pat, you feel like running a message up to the Battlefield?"

"Sure! What you want to tell them?"

"Ask them if they heard the two rifle shots. Tell them if anybody starts anything, I'll fill this cell so full somebody's a cinch to get plugged. Tell them they're welcome to send a couple of their brave boys down here to look the cell over."

"Do you mean that?" Hewitt said, as he saw Pat start for the door.

Pat hesitated. Stambaugh said, "Sure, I mean it! You go with him, if you will, please. But let Pat handle it. You're a reasonable man, Mr. Hewitt, and this is not the time for reason. Let Pat jump on them with both feet, and then help him get back here in one piece."

You, Hewitt decided, are an old fox. . . . He walked through the moonlight with Shane toward the rickety old saloon building. The four or five men lounging in front of the place saw them coming, and flitted inside like startled bats. They yelled their warnings, and the Battlefield suddenly became silent.

It was still quiet when Shane stalked through the door, shouldering it open and then standing there with his thumbs hooked in his belt. Hewitt slipped in behind him and stepped back until he had his back to the wall, beside the door. Shane looked them over contemptuously.

From somewhere near the crowded bar, someone said, "Watch that damned detective. He's a trick shot!" The silence fell again.

Shane said, "This is the last time we'll have trouble from any trail crew in this town. Or from anybody from the shingle mill, either! You mill hands get this good, now. First one of you to show his face in town after tonight, he goes to jail.

"There's two of your riff-raff friends down there in the

jail. Somebody's been standing up on the hill and sharp-shooting into their cell window. Two men can stay out of the way nicely. They won't be hurt, as long as they hide in the corner like the crawling rats they are.

"Marshal Stambaugh says to tell you if there's any trouble out of this bunch tonight, he'll fill that cell so full, somebody will get plugged sure. You yellow bastards can snipe each other off until the cows come home for all I care. Anybody that wants to die a hero, here's his chance."

A hand from the shingle mill, less drunk than the others, and apparently less belligerent, came forward. "Nobody wants trouble with you, Shane," he said. "Just hand over that murdering rapist, and these boys will take care of him for you quietly, and we'll all go home."

Shane had guts, but he lacked the sense of what a crowd was going to do. Hewitt touched him on the shoulder. "Let's go, Pat," he said.

For a moment, he was afraid Pat was going to resent his interference, but he did not. He said, "You mill hands, don't let these saddle bums talk you into trouble. Last warning!"

He turned his back on them and started out the door. The same voice said, more shrilly this time, "Watch that detective! No guns, now! He's a circus shot."

Hewitt slid out behind Shane without turning his back. "Keep going! Don't look back," he said softly to Shane, between his teeth. He stepped to one side and stood with his back against the outside wall, beside the doorway. He slipped the sap from his pocket and transferred it to his left hand, leaving his gun hand free.

A vague shape emerged from the smoky darkness of the Battlefield. The glint of moonlight on his gun told Hewitt where his hand was. Hewitt reached for his wrist, and made a lucky catch. He jerked, spinning the man outside and forcing the arm downward.

The man's wild shot went screaming off down the dusty street. With his left hand, Hewitt jerked the man's arm around his body. He swung the sap lightly, and caught the man in the forehead. He went down on top of his gun. Shane whirled at the sound of the shot.

Another man appeared in the door, both hands in plain sight. Hewitt slid the .45 into his hand and rammed it into the man's stomach. "You had your chance," he said. "Now pick up your pardner here, and carry him down to the jailhouse for us."

"Hell, Mr. Hewitt, I ain't done nothing!" the man quavered, raising his hands.

"You started outside when you should have stayed in your corner. Pick him up, I said!"

"But goddam it, why do I have to go to jail?"

Hewitt jogged him with the gun, and the man groaned a shrill groan and obeyed. He hoisted the unconscious man to his shoulder—a mismatch he would regret, Hewitt thought, hiding a smile. The man being carried outweighed the man carrying him by fifty pounds.

Hewitt picked up the gun the first man had dropped and began walking sidewise down the slope toward the court-house. No one else volunteered to come out the door. He holstered the gun as soon as he felt they were out of side-arm range.

"Got us a couple of volunteers," Shane said to Stam-baugh, holding the door open for the cowboy who came staggering in with the unconscious man over his shoulder. "Some people just won't believe anything they hear."

Stambaugh merely nodded and tossed him the keys. Shane opened the cell. "Inside!" he snarled. The man staggered inside and let his unconscious burden fall to the stone floor. The fallen man groaned and began to mumble as he tried to get to his knees.

The cell door clanged shut violently. "Better get out of

range, Pat," Stambaugh said. "About time for our sharp-
shooting friend to cut loose with one."

Shane stepped aside. "Up against the wall, yander," he
said to the two new prisoners, pointing. "You boys cuddle
up good, now, and maybe nobody will get hit."

Stambaugh signaled Hewitt, Shane, and Godfrey to
come into his office. He closed the door behind them.
"What do you think, Mr. Hewitt?" he said.

"I think if it had been just the cowboys, we could forget
it. Pat put on a hell of a show for them," Hewitt said. "But
with the mill hands . . . I don't know. There's some group
competition now, to see how far they can bait each other
into going."

"My own feeling." Stambaugh nodded. "I hate to see
it come to a shoot-out, but they give us no choice."

"What I want to know," Earl Godfrey rasped, "is where
the hell your volunteer vigilantes is? Seems like now is
when they're needed with their goddam red armbands."

"I don't want any of those old codgers hurt, Mr. Godfrey."

"And you don't care about me, I reckon!"

"You can take pretty good care of yourself. These other
fellows have nerve enough, or they'd never have kept those
armbands on after I came to town."

"This ain't my fight, Marshal. That son of a bitch ain't
my prisoner!"

"You can go any time. Nobody conscripted you."

They were still arguing, the steam going out of Godfrey
in the face of Stambaugh's cool logic, when Hewitt saw
Pat Shane head for the outside door. He slipped out after
him. Shane went to the corner of the building and peered
carefully around it, up toward the Battlefield.

"They're going to try to set fire to the roof," he said.
"What we need is a rifle or two. They're fixing to fire the
roof."

Hewitt dropped to his knees and peered out too. Someone who was not too drunk to think was in charge of the attack, at least at this stage. There was not the usual bloodthirsty talk, by which a mob of lynchers worked themselves up to the point of a blind charge. Somebody up there was using his head.

They had a fire going in a metal wheelbarrow. As Hewitt and Shane watched, someone picked up the handles and started down the street with it. It was the simplest of all military manuevers, an attack on the blind side.

The fire would be wheeled around to the front of the courthouse, and if enough men threw enough burning chunks, some of them would land on the roof and set it afire. The only defense against it meant that the men inside had to come out from behind the rock walls that protected them. Once out of the jail and in the open, they were outnumbered at least ten to one.

"Better tell Stambaugh to bring out the shotguns and the buckshot, Pat. We're going to have to kill a few of them," Hewitt said.

"All right. But God, how I hate to fire on them just to save that murdering ape a hanging!"

He vanished inside. In a moment he came out with Stambaugh and Godfrey. Already, the wheelbarrow full of fire had gone out of sight, and the mob had streamed out of the Battlefield, ready to fight.

Stambaugh handed one shotgun and a box of shells to Godfrey. "You take the other side. Don't challenge them! Just cut loose at their legs with one barrel the minute they come in range. Wait while you count five, and then let them have the other barrel, in the legs. You'll have time to reload then."

He handed the other gun to Shane. "They'll see you the minute you edge out. Wait till you hear Mr. Godfrey fire.

That ought to start something, and maybe give you a chance to get in a shot or two."

"I can feed shells into this thing as fast as you can fire a six-gun," Shane growled.

Stambaugh said wearily, "Just do as you're told. That's all I'll expect of you. Take cover again before you can be hit."

"What," said Hewitt, "are you and I going to be doing?"

"I'll be with Mr. Godfrey, and I expect I'll be able to get in a shot or two after he cuts loose with the buckshot. You're on your own here, Mr. Hewitt."

He turned on his heel and went toward the other back corner, Earl Godfrey at his side. Hewitt peered out and studied the noisy mob up there at the Battlefield. They were still having fun. They had not yet worked up to a killing frenzy.

And whoever was in charge of the wheelbarrow, around in front, had not yet nerved himself to lead a charge on the courthouse. The wheelbarrow was not visible from where Hewitt squatted, but it was plain that the men he was able to see were shouting to encourage someone still too close to them to be dangerous . . . yet. Hewitt touched Shane's shoulder. The big man jumped.

"Pat, when Godfrey opens up, while they're all looking in the other direction, and before you fire, I'm going to break for the stables. If I have to, I can cover you better from there. If I don't have to shoot, I'll be planted there where nobody expects me to be," he said.

"You'll be cut off too. You'll be a dead man, that's what you'll be, once they get onto you," Pat said.

"I think not. We can't possibly throw the lead that they can. We've got to hit them from as many directions as— there he goes!"

The cheerful, drunken yelling up on the street had died down, the rioters holding their breath as the men with the fire-barrow began their charge at the front of the court-house. On the other side of the building, a shotgun roared once.

"He got somebody!" Shane said excitedly. "Oh, listen to the son of a bitch scream!"

"Two of them," Hewitt said, as a second man began howling. "Here I go!"

The shotgun boomed again. Hewitt scuttled across the moonlit space between the courthouse and the sheriff's corral, stooping low. His biggest fear was that Shane, in his excitement, would open fire too soon, and draw attention to him. But when he hit the gatepost and spun around it and looked back, he saw the big deputy marshal waiting phlegmatically.

Hewitt had hit the gatepost harder than he had meant to, running blindly, and it hurt. But the very violence of the impact served to project him into the dubious shelter of the wooden stable. He raised his arm in a signal to Shane.

Shane carefully removed his fine planter's Panama and, just as carefully, laid it behind him in the shelter of the courthouse. He might get hit himself, but he did not mean to have his hat spoiled by bullets. He came out from behind the building like a charging bull, his thick legs moving him with surprising speed.

He ran almost to the front of the courthouse before he stopped, raised the shotgun to his shoulder, and fired. Watching through a crack in the stable wall, Hewitt could see the destruction wrought by the wide pattern of the buckshot, at that maximum range. At least five or six men were hit, and all thought themselves mortally wounded.

Shane fired again, snapped the gun open, fed in two more shells that he held in the palm of his hand, and closed it with a click. He raised it to his shoulder and shot twice more.

He had to fish in his pocket for shells now, and he did so by feel, walking rapidly backward and keeping an eye on the mob. He got his big paw on four more shells, broke the gun, fed two more into the breech. He closed the gun, pulled the two triggers in rapid succession.

He began moving backward again, and now Hewitt could see his face. Shane was grinning like a kid watching the ice-cream freezer being opened at a picnic. He had tumbled a dozen rioters into the dust, considerably reducing their ardor, at least temporarily. Wounded men could still fight, might even be more bloodthirsty once they got to it. But there was always this interim of highly personal pain, and the horrified realization: *Hell, a man could get hurt here!*

Godfrey was methodically firing away on the other side of the courthouse, and Hewitt heard Stambaugh's .45 several times. Shane retreated to cover almost at leisure. The few shots that were thrown at him were at the maximum range of a side arm, and went wild. It was not necessary for Hewitt to betray his presence by firing at all.

They came that close to beating off the lynching party with no worse damage than a few rioters maimed by buckshot.

Then, inside the jail, the four prisoners in the front cell lost their heads and began to scream and shout in panic. They had not been hurt, and had they remained silent, would have been in no danger at all.

But the mob outside heard them. No one had any idea why they screamed. For all the rioters knew, the deputy marshals and the rape-murderer could have been ganging up on them to torture them with knives. The hysterical note in the four voices was all that registered.

It was a blind charge that came down the hill, at least thirty uninjured men who howled their insane rage and held their fire until they could make it count. Well, Hewitt thought, we lost this bet. And it's too bad, because we made a damn good try at it. . . . He stood up and got the .32 out of his shoulder holster, and slipped out of the stable with a gun in each hand.

And just as Pat Shane stood up and made ready to go out and face the mob standing up, with only a double-barreled shotgun, someone began firing a .45 from somewhere the other side of the mob. Another gun joined in, a steady, slow, rhythmic fire, as deadly as it was methodical.

Someone—two voices, in fact—were whooping like Apaches up there. Hewitt shoved the .32 back in his shoulder holster and waved his arm at Shane.

"Come on! They've been hit in the flank. Now's the time to smash them," he shouted.

Shane ran beside him, firing the shotgun on the run, reloading as he ran. "Who in the everlasting *hell!*" he panted; and Hewitt answered, "You don't know them, but I do. Let's just scald these scalawags a little now. We don't need to kill anybody."

The line of tied horses near the saloon had taken all the gunfire they could take. They began to fight, to break their bridles. They ran after the men, and over some of them. Stambaugh and Godfrey appeared, the deputy marshal waving his arms and shouting.

"Hold your fire! Hold your fire, everybody. They won't try it again tonight."

It was over. There were a dozen men left moaning in pain and self-pity on the moonlit grass park in front of the courthouse. Stambaugh called out orders for them to keep their hands away from their guns. "We're going to help you, which is more than you deserve. You're going to be missionaries, boys, preaching how unwise it is to try to take a prisoner away from a United States marshal!"

"I'll be with you in a minute, Mr. Stambaugh," Hewitt said.

He continued on down the street, toward the Y, in the same direction the fleeing lynch mob had taken as it broke up. Two tall, straight-standing men stepped out of the shadows. Around them hung the unmistakable odor of powder smoke.

"At ease, boys," Hewitt said. "You hit them just in time. They had us boxed in."

Mac chuckled. "When you start firing at their tails as they charge, you change their minds mighty sudden. 'Twasn't nothing for a couple of old sojers, Mr. Hewitt."

"I know that, boys, but we appreciate it, anyway. What can we do for you in return?"

"We want some money down, before we dynamite that fill," Toby said.

"Nonsense! You fellows are out of trouble now—why not stay that way?"

"No, sir, by God! You said you could get us fifty dollars."

"I'm sure I can, if you insist on this folly, but—"

"But, hell! We've got eighteen charges laid, all set to fire. They're all on one-hour fuses, and we'll be back in our bunks before they go off. But we're entitled to half of the money in advance."

Hewitt thought it over. "Not quite half. I'll advance you ten each out of my own funds, and I'll get you the rest to-morrow—*if that road is gone!* But you understand that I can't have anything to do with it myself. It's a crime, a—"

"You just come up with some money, Mr. Hewitt. We don't need no lectures."

He gave them each ten dollars. "Now we need a cigar, too," Mac said. "Only way you can touch off that many fuses in a row is with a cigar. And then we'll have to go like hell to get back to the tent. I only hope we ain't already been missed."

Hewitt gave them a cigar and matches to light it. "Better still," he said, "as soon as you have touched off your fuses, hurry back here. I'll throw you both in jail for the night."

"Well what a hell of a way to treat—"

"It's the best alibi you can have, boys, if you're locked up in jail when those shots go off. We'll have to let you go at daylight, though, because someone fires a rifle into that cell every morning."

"You're a real friend, Mr. Hewitt," Toby said warmly. "You think of everything, don't you?"

CHAPTER NINE

It was exactly 3:00 A.M. when Hewitt herded his two new prisoners into the back door of the bottom floor of the courthouse.

Stambaugh, exhausted, had gone to sleep with his boots on. Pat Shane had received two wounds that he had not felt until it was over. Both were shallow flesh wounds in his left side, where .45 bullets had skated through the skin and surface fat just under it. He was sitting on Hewitt's bunk, sleepily plastering them with pine-tar horse salve.

"Sh-h!" he said, nodding toward Stambaugh. Hewitt nodded and mouthed, "The keys!" Shane pointed to the end of Stambaugh's bunk, where Stambaugh had dropped them.

Hewitt took Toby and Mac to the cell that was still occupied by the four cowboys arrested earlier in the night. Shane, cursing his wounds under his breath, got up and came into the corridor to see what was going on.

"I tried to throw them out, but they don't think so much of freedom now," he whispered. "Safest place in town for them until things cool off."

Hewitt unlocked and opened the cell door. "Inside, and better hug the far wall, boys," he said. "Whoever is close to the door is likely to get hit by a rifle slug come morning."

Toby and Mac brutally kicked the sleeping cowboys out of the way, and took over the safest part of the cell. Hewitt

and Shane returned to the big bullpen cell, closing its door
to the corridor behind them.

Stambaugh half sat up. "What's doing?" he mumbled.

"I just threw a couple of rock heads in for the night,"
Hewitt replied.

"What did they do?"

"It's what they didn't do. They wouldn't go home."

"What time is it?"

"Must be close to two in the morning."

"I have barely been asleep, then. I'll try to catch a little
more, if you can take the watch."

"You do that, Mr. Stambaugh. I'm fine."

"I had never yet lost a prisoner to a mob, and it was
tried on me twice. That's one reason I was sent here. My
luck held this night, Mr. Hewitt," Stambaugh said. And
promptly went to sleep again.

Shane yanked out his fat silver watch. Hewitt caught
his eye and shook his head vigorously: No, no, no! Shane
pocketed the watch with a shrug that said, all right, if you
insist, it's only two o'clock.

Thirty-some minutes later, the charges in the rock fill
under the road began to go off. Hewitt counted them, and
was surprised when number 17 went off—still more surprised to count number 18. It was a good powder-monkey
who got 100 per cent out of that many loads.

Stambaugh did not wake up, but Shane looked more
and more puzzled as the cannonade went on and on and
on. "That don't sound like it's out to the quarry," he
whispered to Hewitt. "That's a hell of a lot of dynamite,
and it sounded real close."

"Maybe you ought to take a look," said Hewitt, with a
yawn.

Shane studied him suspiciously for a moment. "I reckon
maybe you're right," he said, and went out.

Daylight was filtering into Kaylee's Ford when he returned. Hewitt had made a pot of coffee without arousing Stambaugh, and was on his first cup. Stambaugh awakened when Shane clumped in, inwardly aquiver with excitement.

"Somebody blew the hell out of that fill where the road crosses Bear Creek," he reported.

In the cell across the corridor, Toby and Mac snored loudly, sleeping the sleep of the just.

"Blew the road up?" Stambaugh said, trying to come awake.

"I do hope to tell you, they blew it up! Regular old flood went down the channel to Kaylee's Creek. That is some of the worst-stinking goddam water you ever smelled, Lee!"

Stambaugh tottered to his feet. "Let me have that again. What happened?"

Shane told him. "Whoever laid them loads knowed what he was doing. He just picked that fill up and laid it over on the edge of Kaylee's Creek. What's there now is just a big, stinking hole in the ground. They shouldn't be allowed to build that road there again."

"They won't be," Stambaugh said quietly. He got up and went over and poured himself a cup of coffee. He looked sleepily at Hewitt. "This solves your problem of moving that road, doesn't it?"

"It would seem so," Hewitt said. "Remarkable coincidence, but then life is full of coincidences."

"Lately, anyway. You going to go have a talk with Mr. Edwin W. Newhart-Poulton now?"

"I wonder if it won't be unnecessary. I wonder if Mr. Newhart-Poulton won't come here."

"It's possible. He doesn't impress me as a man who takes much stock in coincidence."

Hewitt nodded. "My feeling too. If you're awake enough take a strain on things, I'll try to sleep now."

"Go ahead. I'll wake you up if I need you."

"I think I'll stay awake a while," said Shane.

Hewitt took off his boots and stretched out fully dressed on his bunk. He woke up enough to hear the argument between Stambaugh and Newhart-Poulton a little later when the sun was higher.

"What kind of bumpkin do you think I am? Hewitt threatens me explicitly, and in a matter of hours his threat is carried out," said Newhart-Poulton.

"Mr. Newhart-Poulton, if you mean that you suspect Mr. Hewitt of blowing up your road, I personally can account for every minute of his time last night. In case you can't be bothered to keep up with community news of a trivial nature, we had an attempted lynching here last night," said Stambaugh.

"I know all about that. I want to know where those two rock heads are that he was talking to yesterday, when I came upon him in the quarry. He made his threat in their presence. Find them, deputy marshal, and I'm sure you'll have the bombers."

"I don't know anything about that, and I'm too busy this morning to care much. I've got six men in the jail, and if you want to look them over, help yourself."

Apparently Newhart-Poulton helped himself. "Why, damn it, you've already got them! Those are the chaps who blew up the road, that one, and that one."

"Nobody in that cell blew up anything. Those four men have been in since daylight yesterday. Those two came in at exactly two in the morning."

"Nonsense! Those charges were set with long fuses. Thirty feet of fuse, which burns a foot a minute. There's enough fuse left, with its core burned out, to tell a man as experienced as myself exactly what happened."

"Mr. Newhart-Poulton, when did that dynamite go off? About three-thirty, wasn't it? Those two men had been in jail an hour and a half then."

"Providing them," Newhart-Poulton said cuttingly,

"with an extremely convenient alibi. Please don't treat me like a country boy."

"Are you calling me a liar?"

"Are you calling me one too? I took my watch out when Mr. Hewitt brought those prisoners in," Shane said. He did not bother to add that its hands had stood at three.

"I know when I've been hornswoggled. I can take a defeat. I've got to build my road by the other route, and since it's going to take several days, I may as well get at it. But it galls me, deputy, it downright *galls* me, to have that man, Hewitt, trick me. There, sir, is the most arrogant man I have ever known!"

"He says the same thing about you, but listen, Mr. Newhart-Poulton," Stambaugh said, "this is really to your benefit too. After last night's trouble, this town isn't going to be very tolerant of outsiders. You'll cut a much better figure, when your new road . . ."

Hewitt dozed off. Shane woke him up when the station agent came with a telegram. "It don't make sense to me, Mr. Hewitt," the agent apologized, "but I took it just the way it came over. I ain't the best operator in the world, and I hated to ask him to repeat such a short message. But it just don't make sense to me."

Hewitt read the telegram, which said:

ASK ASA WISNER WHY SODAK.

"It makes sense to me," Hewitt said, folding the wire and tucking it into his shirt pocket. "Later today—not much later, come to think of it—I'll want to file a fairly long telegram. Can you rush it for me?"

The agent practically wrung his hands. "I been feeling poorly the last few days. I hope you won't mind if I get Mrs. Patterson to handle your telegram. I need a couple of days off, I need it real bad!"

"Quite satisfactory, and this is for your kindness in rushing this to me," Hewitt said.

He tipped the agent a dollar and was grateful again for the subtle and frugal mind of Conrad Meuse, who could stuff two separate messages into five words, without having to pay the higher rate for code. The apparently straightforward message from Conrad actually consisted of two separate items of intelligence.

The first, ASK ASA WISNER, referred Hewitt to a Chicago detective with whom Bankers' Bonding & Indemnity Company had often co-operated before. That told Hewitt where the Pedisquod Hotel was.

The other two words, WHY SODAK, could be translated as, "Why are you in South Dakota?" I wonder myself, Hewitt thought. Have to think up a reason to soothe Conrad. . . .

Shane could have gone back to his room at Mrs. Stillman's and slept the day away, but he could not bear to be away from the scene of any possible excitement. He fell asleep on Stambaugh's bunk, and slept deeply despite his wounds.

Hewitt spent the better part of an hour composing a long wire to Asa Wisner, crossing out words, combining words, suggesting lines of inquiry to a detective who resented suggestions. When he was through, there was nothing in it that Asa Wisner could object to—and no mention of the Pedisquod Hotel, either.

He saddled Rowdy, after Earl Godfrey had brought the horses back and fed them. He took time to shave. He meant to stop for breakfast with Myra Green, but when he got there, the place was closed. Someone had thrown a rock through the window—one weighing more than fifty pounds.

The quarrymen who were not welcome there had registered their resentment. Myra was not the only one to have closed up for the morning. Across the street, Merle

Johnco's shop had not opened; neither had the small grocery store down the street, nor the shoe repairman next to it.

The riot at the courthouse and the dynamiting of the quarry road had made people cautious. Hewitt saw two men wearing armbands. They saluted him in a friendly manner, but without undue display. He returned their greetings respectfully. They were glad not to have been pulled into last night's shoot-out, and he did not blame them.

The ford where Captain Kaylee had made local history was running at its normal level and the water had cleared up, but the high-water mark showed where the dammed-up, stagnant waters above the rock fill had gone through. It had narrowly missed overflowing the banks and running down the street past Myra Green's restaurant.

He crossed the ford and rode to the Patterson place. One of the Patterson boys told him that his mother had been called to run the railroad station this morning when the agent became ill. He rode there and found the woman busy at her bookwork.

"I declare, he lets everything go until it's such a mess he can't tell north from south!" she fretted. "Then he takes down sick, and I have to straighten it out."

"One of the penalties of virtue is that those who have it must supply it for those who lack it, Roma," Hewitt said.

She chuckled heartily. "I'll bet there's a lot of wisdom in that, if I could just get my hands on it. I see you got an answer to your wire. Everything all right?"

"Just fine. I'd like this one to go out as soon as you have time. I hope I get an answer yet today."

"If you do, I'll get it to you. Wire's open now. Let's get this on the way," she said briskly.

She moved to the instrument and closed her switch. She

spread Hewitt's message out and sounded her dispatching
signal on the key. She then sent the "hold" signal and
turned to look at Hewitt, who still leaned on the counter.

"Mr. Hewitt, just what does this mean?" she demanded.

"That's information I have to have."

"My God!"

He said earnestly, "Don't jump to conclusions, Roma.
There mustn't be any gossip. I want you to forget this as
soon as you've got it on the wire."

"That's more than you can ask of me." She took a handkerchief from her pocket and wiped her eyes. "I—I just
get to where I'm healed, to where I'm content to leave her
in God's hands, and then something like this brings her
face back to me."

"It will probably always be that way," Hewitt said
gently, "but I think soon it will stop aching so much, and
to remember her will be a blessing, not a torment. What
we have to do is clear up all this confusion, and give you
and Nate a little peace."

"We don't want any more mobs like last night!" she
said. She blew her nose vigorously. "Who's going to pay
you for this, Mr. Hewitt? I've heard you get huge pay. Nate
and I can't. You're welcome to what—"

He cut in, "It's paid for. I owe this much to Deputy
Marshal Stambaugh."

"It's wonderful, how a detective deduces things."

"No. It's a dull business of trial and error, actually. You
choose your most likely suspect and try to prove he did it.
Sometimes, all you do is prove he could not possibly have
done it. You go on to somebody else and repeat the
process.

"The most troublesome cases are those with a lot of
suspects, a lot of whom have already left town. I'd guess
that there have been twenty men coming into this town,
and twenty going out, every day since the quarry opened.

That's why we've got to grub, grub, grub, like looking for a ring you lost while weeding your garden. That's why I have to send wires like this."

"Let's get it off," she said.

She turned to her telegraph key and began sending his message. Hewitt could send and receive a little, but Roma Patterson was one of the most skillful operators he had ever seen. He was not surprised when the relay man to Chicago cut in and signaled her to repeat.

Two cowboys, mere kids that he had never seen before, were walking tired horses across the ford when he reached the creek. They had no way of knowing about last night's shoot-out, and how unwelcome it had made them in Kaylee's Ford. He spurred Rowdy ahead to catch up with them and pass on a friendly warning.

Then he saw the face of one, and thought, let him find out for himself. . . . The other one was an ordinary drifter, one of the witless, chinless, unambitious youths who drifted westward to escape minor trouble at home, and were never quite out of minor trouble wherever they went. But the one with a vest on, and no sleeves in his shirt, was one of the mean-eyed, aggressive young hellions who so often were responsible for major troubles.

He followed them. They took the left-hand fork of the Y, some fifty feet ahead of him. They tied in front of the meat market, which had a sign out, FRESH VEAL TODAY. Hewitt tied Rowdy not far away and went into the market. He was pretty sure it was not fresh veal that had caught the two young riders' eyes.

There were three older women in the market—and Merle Johnco. No doubt the two had seen her turn in before tying there. He tipped his hat to her.

"Good morning, ma'am. If I may, I'll walk you part of the way home. You have a couple of admirers outside," he said.

She glanced quickly at the window and then back again. The two young cowboys had been looking in. They looked away quickly, and lounged nonchalantly against the wall.

"It isn't necessary at all," she said coolly. "Thank you, but I can take care of myself."

He nodded, smiled, and replaced his hat. "Of course, Mrs. Johnco, whatever you say. Although I doubt if you know cowboys. I'll be nearby, just in case."

"I would rather you did not."

He went outside and stood near Rowdy, waiting. The two cowboys sized him up: One man, to them an "old" one, and a dude besides—forget him! They did not talk, but they watched the market door like hawks. Or, Hewitt thought, like young toughs who had spent a lonesome winter snowed in on a cow ranch somewhere, Canada probably, and had left what little judgment they had up there. . . .

The door opened. The two tensed a little. One of the older women came out. The two relaxed. Again the door opened, again it was one of the older women; again the two young drifters nonchalantly picked their teeth with their thumbnails and yawned at the sky.

Merle Johnco came out carrying a tiny packet of veal. She passed Hewitt without a look, but he thought she was a little unsure of herself, having seen the two at the door. Head up, she started the long, hot walk—at least a quarter of a mile up a shallow, breathless, tree-shaded canyon—to her isolated house.

About twenty feet behind her came the two cowboys. Hewitt fell in about the same distance behind them. It was hard for him to blame them too much. The sight of a woman as attractive as Mrs. Johnco could disturb the judgment of many an older man.

Ordinarily, your drifting cowboy was a rather shy country lad, where decent women were concerned. One of these was probably just like that—the one with the blue shirt. It was the one with the vest would be the trouble-maker, the one to watch.

They left the last store behind, and soon the last house. The woman had no idea Hewitt was behind her, and how hard it must be to maintain this slow, steady pace! Her instinct would be to run, but she would know that this would only force the two riders to a showdown.

Denim Vest dug his elbow into Blue Shirt's ribs and leaned over to say something to him. Blue Shirt did not respond, and he increased his pace reluctantly to keep up with his friend. Hewitt stepped out faster still. He was not six feet behind them when they split and fell into step with Mrs. Johnco, one on each side.

"Hello, dearie," said Denim Vest. "Long way from home, ain't you? Like a little company, dearie?"

Why, Hewitt thought, fool around . . . ? He made his jump and caught Blue Shirt by the collar and hauled him backward. The kid blatted like a sheep in surprise and terror. Hewitt kicked a leg out from under him and let him drop.

Where he dropped was against his own friend, and Hewitt grabbed at the same time. He knew he was being warned when Denim Vest came around with both fists cocked, the left out, the right hugged back against the ribs and the jaw tucked back against the left shoulder.

"Some other time, we can do it your way," Hewitt said. "Not today, though." He slipped the sap from his pocket, feinted at Denim Vest's face with it. Denim Vest's left shot out, to come in under the sap. Hewitt snapped his wrist and caught the thick, hard biceps with it, and just before that deadly right could come around in a short hook, he rapped the kid just above the nose with the sap.

All he had meant to do was slow the kid down, let him stand there swaying, while agony throbbed through his whole left arm. He got more contact than he wanted. He saw Denim Vest's eyes roll up. His knees buckled, wide apart. He twisted and went down inertly.

Hewitt caught Blue Shirt by the shoulders and hauled him to his feet. "No guns, son," he said. "Let's see both hands, wide open."

"I ain't going for no gun," the kid quavered.

Hewitt kept hold of his shoulders and shook him hard. "Why do you let that scum talk you into things like this? Can't you tell a decent woman when you see one?"

"We didn't mean no harm. We was only—"

Hewitt slapped him. "Don't lie to me! I heard you getting smart with this lady. Do you want to take your sidekick and ride right on out of town, or would you like a month on a county road gang?"

The kid looked down at Denim Vest. "He'll kill me, first chance. God, you don't know how mean he is, mister!"

"Then fog it out of here without him. This is your chance to be rid of him. Start riding and keep riding, and let him cool his own saucer of coffee. What's your name, kid?"

"Clark, sir. Alden Clark."

"What's his?"

"Pearl De Freese, only don't call him 'Pearl.' He hates that name. He likes to be called 'Mickey.'"

"Get going! Pearl's going to have a nice nap, and then cool off in a cell. You can put twenty miles between you, if you try."

Alden Clark was fully persuaded. He started back toward his horse at a shambling trot. Hewitt looked at the woman, who had waited quietly a few steps away.

"I think I had better overrule you, ma'am, and see you home now."

She thanked him with a nod and fell into step with him. Neither spoke. When her house was in sight, Hewitt paused and looked back. Only one figure was in sight and it had not moved. He lifted his hat.

"You'll be all right now, Mrs. Johnco. I'll go take care of yonder Sleeping Beauty."

"No, let me give you a cup of tea first. I'm so ashamed of the way I behaved. I heard who you are, and I'm afraid I'm prejudiced against detectives."

"Most people are," he said, smiling. "How long since I've been offered a cup of tea! It will be a pleasure, ma'am."

She met his eyes. "I'm sorry. That's all I can say."

"And it's more than you should say. It's a filthy game I'm in, but I never take a filthy case. No man is guiltless, the Bible says. But what guilt I bear, I don't owe to my job."

"But—but they say—"

"Go on, ma'am, what do they say?"

"That you're here to build a hanging case against that poor, ignorant, tongue-tied quarryman. There's nothing against him except circumstantial evidence and blind, ugly, stupid, hateful prejudice."

"Yes, that's what Mr. Stambaugh tells me."

"*What?*"

"Surprises you? Don't let this go any further, ma'am, but Stambaugh sent for me to find the murderer, *not* to convict his prisoner. He doesn't think he's guilty."

"But my husband takes food to Tcherin. It's a constant struggle to get in with it."

"No one likes his jail interfered with in my business, but your husband's problem is with Shane, and he doesn't run the jail. Neither of you must discuss it with anyone— I can't insist too strongly on that. But don't be mistaken about our motives."

Her eyes filled suddenly with tears. She opened the door and went in ahead of him. He followed her into a big, stark room with only an old couch, an old rocking chair, and a small willow-work table. Four oil paintings leaned against the wall; two were of Mrs. Johnco.

She saw him looking at the paintings. "My husband paints. If you'll please sit down, I'll be only a minute," she said distractedly.

She went into the kitchen and he heard her starting the oil-stove fire under the teakettle. He sat down on one end of the couch. A folded quilt, a folded Indian blanket, and a pillow were stacked neatly on the floor beside him.

He studied the paintings. There was a landscape he liked very much, a tall, narrow, vertical view down the path through the trees from the front stoop. It had been painted in early fall, when the leaves were starting to turn, and it had something both lonely and peaceful in it. A man who found that prospect from his front door could be a happy man indeed.

There was a still-life of the old willow-work table with a small clock, a pair of Mrs. Johnco's gloves, and what seemed to be an ornate Valentine card. It puzzled Hewitt by its pervasive gloominess. It occurred to him that it was both a later picture than the landscape and an unhappier one.

One of the portraits of Mrs. Johnco was quite formal, a small one showing her face only, with a blue veil thrown back. The man had worked hard on this one, and it was a good likeness, yet without emotional impact.

The other portrait was larger, and it was all emotion and vivid, intoxicating sunlight and flowers. It showed her bare shoulders and just the start of the swell of that magnificent bust. Her hair was in braids wound carelessly around her head, and there was something about her expression that excited him strangely.

Then it came to him: This one had been painted outdoors, in the nude. There was probably a full figure painted at the same time, somewhere, and Johnco had copied the head only because it was too good to keep hidden, even in this small, bucolic town. I wish I could see the other one, Hewitt thought . . . and had to swallow hard.

She came in with a tray holding a plain earthenware teapot, cups, and a plate of small sandwiches. "I have let us run out of sugar again. Can you drink it without?" she said with that same curious air of distraction.

He lied. "I always take it that way, ma'am."

Pouring the tea, sitting in the rocker opposite him, seemed to restore her poise. She asked him how he liked Kaylee's Ford; she said that she and her husband liked it despite the depressing blight of the murder, and the quarry; she thought all four seasons were good here, and she did not mind the cold of winter at all.

He changed the subject deliberately. "I've been studying your husband's paintings. I dabble at it, you know. He's very good, isn't he?"

She raised one eyebrow but refused to be baited into resuming their discussion about dabbling. "He's extremely gifted, but untrained. His father objected to art, and would barely consent to his studying music."

"Oh? What instrument does he play?"

"Everything. He gave it up years ago and has no instrument of his own now. There's a good organ in the church here, and that's his best instrument. He has been playing on afternoons when no one is at the church—more and more lately."

"What church is that?"

"The Methodist."

He looked at his watch. "I've run out of time, ma'am."

"It was so kind of you to help me, and I deserved it so little. I hope you'll come back, Mr. Hewitt, and talk painting with my husband."

He stood up and picked his hat up off the couch. "I believe I'll keep his respect, and not mention art, Mrs. Johnco. I work in crayons, that's all."

He walked toward the door. She went with him. He opened the door. She said, "No, really, I'm sure you're better than that. Please come back! There's no one here for Adrian to talk to—or for me to talk to, for that matter."

She offered him her hand. He took it, held it, and said, "If I do, will you show me that other picture?"

"What other picture?"

"The one like that," he said, nodding toward the portrait of her with bare shoulders.

She looked around at it and looked back at him quickly. Her eyes narrowed slightly, and she said, "I might. Good afternoon, Mr. Hewitt, and thank you again."

CHAPTER TEN

Hewitt, walking swiftly, was a block and a half from the house before he had control of his breath back. By God, now, I must take no more chances there! he scolded himself. . . . There was something unsettled about Mrs. Johnco, something wild, headstrong, and stubborn, as well as a strong and appealing tincture of plain fright.

She talked too much about her husband. (The lady doth protest too much, methinks!) A woman who had got herself into one unhappy alliance too recklessly, often became too reckless in escaping into another, equally unhappy. Certainly, Merle Johnco was no offhand trifler. You would, as the saying went, have her on your hands.

Denim Vest, or Pearl De Freese, or even Mickey as he liked to call himself, was plodding sedately down the path ahead, still not quite sure of his footing. He was also suffering from an aching left arm that would be sorer still tomorrow.

Hewitt caught up with him, caught him by the bare arm. "Come on, podner, we're going to take a walk," he said.

De Freese shook off Hewitt's hand. He knew better than to take a poke at Hewitt in his present condition, but he did not mean to go peacefully. Hewitt let go of the arm, and when De Freese relaxed, he grabbed at it again, this time at the wrist.

He twisted the hand back into the small of De Freese's back. "You've already got one bad wing," he said. "I can put this one out of commission for a few weeks if I have to. Let's go."

He leaned around his prisoner, to take the gun from his holster. He put it in his own back pants pocket and walked De Freese faster.

"You kin let go. I'll come along," De Freese said.

"You bet your life you will!"

Hewitt let go of the wrist. He stayed half a step back of De Freese, keeping a little to the man's right. The more he saw of him, the less he liked him.

They came to the two horses—first Rowdy, and then the handsome little bay De Freese had ridden. De Freese said nothing about his missing partner, but he started to turn toward his horse.

"No, it's a short walk. I'll come back for our horses, podner," Hewitt said.

De Freese turned to face him. "What the hell! You ain't really gonna throw me in no jail, now."

"Don't you bet on it. Let's go."

"What for? We didn't say nothing dirty to the lady."

"Got a lot of other things to talk about. Let's go."

De Freese faced him without fear. "You've got the edge now. I hafta go with you. But you watch me get turned out, and when I do, you and me is going to settle it between us. Just you and me."

"Let's wait until then to talk about it. *I said, let's go!*"

De Freese turned. His head was clearer now. He walked more steadily, and he walked like a trained fighting animal, on the balls of his feet, leaning slightly forward. He was no taller than Hewitt, but he was magnificently built and broad of shoulder. There was not an ounce of fat or soft flesh in his more than one hundred and eighty pounds.

The Battlefield, when they passed it, was closed; it had not opened at all today. They crossed the courthouse grounds in a blazing sun. Lee Stambaugh, freshly shaved, was just coming out of the door to throw out a basin of soapy water.

"Is the front cell empty?" Hewitt asked him.

"Yes. I threw your two men out along with mine. No use being too technical, when we've made our point."

"I've got a customer for you."

Stambaugh looked De Freese over. "What's he in trouble for?"

"Tell you about it later." Hewitt jogged De Freese in the back with his thumb. "Let's go. Right on through here, and through that door. First cell to the right."

The cell door stood open. De Freese went into it willingly enough, but he turned with that tigerish quickness that seemed to be built into him, as Hewitt closed the door and then clinched the padlock in the big sliding hasp. Hewitt went to the next cell.

Adrian Johnco had already paid Tcherin his daily visit. There were two sandwiches on Tcherin's bunk, but he had not touched them. He had retreated into his tight little world of fear, and was shuffling back and forth in the cell. If he heard or saw Hewitt, he gave no sign.

Hewitt went to the small office, where Stambaugh was preparing to take a bath. The door to the bathroom stood open, and a fire roared in the water heater. Hewitt said in a low voice, "Like to talk to you a minute."

Stambaugh nodded. "While I soak."

"Where's Pat? I'd just as soon there were someone here to keep an eye on my prisoner."

"Gone to eat."

"It can wait, then. I want to do a little thinking, anyway."

Hewitt went into the bullpen cell, and sat down in the chair, where he could see the open door. De Freese was not visible, but Hewitt could hear him moving about in the cell.

"De Freese!" he called.

"What?"

"Better stay back against the far wall, there. Don't come close to the bars."

"Why not?"

"There's a sharpshooter who usually takes a few shots into the window of that cell, during the day sometime. If you're back against the masonry wall, you're safe."

"This is a hell of a note. Who is he?"

"No idea."

The cell door jangled, as though De Freese had shaken it. "Get me out of here, then! You can't leave a man in here to be bushwhacked through the winder."

"You won't be bushwhacked if you stay back from the bars. If you're standing up by the door, though, you're right in the line of fire."

A muttered oath, the sound of movement, and De Freese apparently got out of the line of fire. Hewitt waited. In a few minutes, De Freese's voice came again, this time from the rear of the cell:

"What kinda gun does he shoot?"

"If we knew that, we might know who he is."

"How big a slug?"

"I've got a fair idea, but there's not much left of them by the time they hit."

"How fur a shot is it?"

"De Freese, let's wait until we see how much information you come up with, before I start telling you what we know."

"I don't know nothing. I ain't done nothing to be in jail. Where's my sidekick, what did you do with him? You got no right to keep me in your crumby jail."

Hewitt put a fresh pot of coffee on Stambaugh's little spirit stove while he tried to figure out where De Freese came from by his speech. His accent was a queer combination. Mostly it was rural Southwest, but with certain intonations and turns of speech that sounded like New York.

De Freese was a natural fighter, one of those men born with the lightning reflexes and the natural punch that needed only polishing, not teaching. "Mickey" was a favorite ring name. Say a homesteader's trouble-making son, a runaway from Kansas or Colorado to try his luck in the club fights in New York.

Then what? Not good enough—or not honest enough—to get into the big money. Hewitt could easily imagine De Freese throwing a fight for ten dollars that he could have won for fifty. He had the innate avarice and stupid guile that would cause him to lean to the crooked dollar instinctively.

Stambaugh, in fresh, clean clothing, came into the room. Hewitt threw him a signal with his eyes, and they went into the outer, empty office, closing the door to the jail. There being no place to sit here, they conferred standing up in low voices.

"Who is your prisoner?" Stambaugh's face creased in one of his rare smiles. "You can't throw a man in jail on his looks, but if you could, he'd be my first one."

"He's just as nice as he looks, too. I may have made a bad blunder, Mr. Stambaugh."

"That doesn't sound like you."

Hewitt told him how he had caught De Freese and his partner accosting Mrs. Johnco. "I put this one away with my cosh, and hit him a little harder than I meant. No regrets, you understand—that's just how it happens he was still there afterward."

"After what?"

"After I had run his sidekick out of town and taken Mrs. Johnco home. She felt it necessary to ask me in for a cup of tea. That's a politeness I felt I could not turn down. I figured this fellow would be long gone and far away, when

I came out of the Johnco house. But, as I say, I must have hit him a pretty good one. He was just on his feet, but not very steady on them, when I caught up with him.

"I was just going to give him a fast start out of town, too, but he wanted to fight. His partner seemed to be happy to be rid of him, and I thought that a night in jail for this fellow would give the partner a nice running start, as well as teach this boy his manners.

"That's all I had in mind, Mr. Stambaugh—just a night in the brine, to bring out the best in him. But once I started him on the way, I never once had to tell him how to get here. He knows this town! He knows it well, and has been here before.

"Now I wish I had his partner too. I think he would be a faster talker; this fellow can be tough. Now I ask myself *when* this fellow was here before, and *what* he was doing then, and *why* he came back. And if he knows the people as well as he knows the town—why get gay with Mrs. Johnco? Who is he? And I don't mean just his name and the size of his hat and socks."

Stambaugh had not lost his look of interest, but all trace of good humor was gone from his face. "I don't see how Mrs. Johnco comes into it, at all. She can't be blamed if she was accosted on the street."

"That's the point. This fellow isn't bright, but he's rat-smart and he was stone sober. What made him think he could get away with it in broad daylight—especially after the kind of night we had here? Everybody in town is on edge and suspicious. I assumed they had ridden into town not knowing of the trouble we had. But if he knows the town—if he was bold enough to come in anyway and make himself unpleasant to Mrs. Johnco on the street—"

"He's got a lot of questions to answer." Stambaugh thought it over grimly. "It just doesn't sound like your work, though, Mr. Hewitt."

"What doesn't?"

"Why, to whip those two men and leave them at liberty.
I'd think you would have jailed them both. If any saddle
bum thinks he can ride into this town and accost a decent
woman on the street—"

"I knew Mrs. Johnco didn't want to make a fuss; and
when I whipped them and left them at liberty, as you say,
I didn't know this fellow was familiar with the town. Beyond that, all I can say is that when you're with Mrs.
Johnco, and for some time afterward, all you can think
about is Mrs. Johnco."

Something spread across Stambaugh's face and came
to quick, hot focus in his eyes, and Hewitt thought, Why,
poor devil, he's in love with her! He can't have known her
longer than six weeks, and he's half out of his mind over
her. . . . It was yearning and jealousy and a sudden, vicious, burning hatred that glittered out of Stambaugh's
secretive eyes.

Then the deputy marshal seemed to get hold of himself.
It was as though he sent Hewitt a message with a look: *All
right, you've caught me, but never mention it again, and
never speak lightly of the woman to me. . . .*

"What do you want to do, Mr. Hewitt? You can hold
him a day or two, but the books will have to show some
kind of serious charge. I've got to account to a United
States judge, sooner or later."

"First, I want to question him, and—"

Hewitt's nerves were more on edge than he had thought.
The rifle bullet smacked into the wooden box in the corner,
both men jumped, and that nerve-racking shriek seemed
to keep echoing long after it was over. It made him remember how badly he needed a rest.

"I don't think you want to question him in his cell,
though," Stambaugh said.

The twinkle was back in his eyes. Hewitt smiled and

said, "No, in here is better, but let's wait until Pat gets back."

"Why?"

"Mr. Stambaugh, take my word for it, this is a dangerous man. I'd like to have him in an Oregon boot as long as we've got him here."

"And yet you walked off and left him, out cold on the sidewalk!"

"And let his partner get away. I wish I had him back, but it would be a waste of time to go after him."

They stood there a moment, sizing each other up. It was as though they were waiting for the next sharpshooter's shot to come, and get that business settled, before going on to the next item on the agenda.

It came, but they were both prepared for the shriek and thud. Neither moved. From the cell where Pearl De Freese was locked, however, came the thud and rattle as he kicked the bars and then jumped back out of the line of fire.

"Hey, I want a lawyer!" De Freese snarled.

"Wouldn't do you any good," said Hewitt. "There are no judges in town to grant writs. Just sit back against the rock wall and meditate on your sins."

De Freese kicked the door again and yelled, "You put me in here to let some son of a bitch kill me, goddam you to hell! I get out of here, ain't no place on this goddam earth you can hide from me."

Stambaugh whispered, "He's getting snaky."

Hewitt whispered back, "Let him sweat a few more minutes. He might talk after all."

"What are you sonsabitches whispering about?" De Freese shouted.

They did not answer. This would have been a good moment for another rifle shot, but none came.

"Hey, this ape in the next cell, he ain't got no clothes on!" De Freese yelled. "What's he in for? Make him stop walking. What the hell kind of a place is this, you put me in with some kind of a baboon that hasn't even got any clothes on and let them shoot at me!"

"They're not shooting at you, Pearl," Hewitt said. "They're shooting at him."

"What did you call me?" Hewitt did not answer. De Freese went on, "Make him put some clothes on. What the hell kind of a jail is this? Look, he don't even hear me, he just keeps on walking, what kind of a baboon is he?"

Someone was approaching the rear of the courthouse, whistling Sailor's Hornpipe expertly. "Anybody to home?" Pat Shane called, coming in the back door. "By golly, if this ain't the coolest place in town, I'll eat your shirt right off'n your back."

"Watch yourself," Stambaugh said. "We've had two shots through the window."

"Whoo-*ee!*" Shane darted inside with a speed surprising in his clumsy bulk.

Across the corridor, De Freese called to him, "Hey, you! Let me out of here. You look like a man that would give a fella an even break. Make these hayseeds let me out of their goddam jail."

Shane took off his fine planter's hat and fanned himself with it. He cocked an eye at Stambaugh. "Who is that?" he said. And then, without waiting for an answer, he went on, "Jeff, this is going to tickle you plumb to death. I met Mr. Newhart-Poulton, and he said he wants to see you up at his office by four this afternoon."

"What did you tell him?"

"I said if he wanted to see you to come down here and we'd try to make an appointment. He didn't say what was bothering him, but I reckon it's his road. I heard at the table today he's made a deal to cross Nate Patterson's land with a new road."

"Shut up and listen, Pat," Stambaugh said in a low voice.

"Pat, we've got a prisoner here that may know quite a bit that we ought to know. Mr. Stambaugh and I are going to bring him in here to question him," Hewitt said, almost in a whisper.

Shane continued to fan himself, but he looked serious. Hewitt went on: "This is a bad one. We want you here in the room with us, and don't take it lightly because three are none too many with this one. He's smart, he's scared, he's vicious, and he's quick as a cat. Haven't you got a gun?"

"Pshaw, a pistol? I'd just shoot myself with it!"

"Are those shotguns still around?"

"Under Lee's desk."

"All right, get one of them, make sure it's loaded, and then you had better bring the chair in from the little office, and sit right there. I'll bring this fellow in, and let him sit on Mr. Stambaugh's bed."

"Why mine?" said Stambaugh.

Hewitt explained patiently. "If Pat has to shoot, I want the stone wall behind our target, not this damned thin wood with Tcherin beyond it."

"All right. I see there's a right way and a wrong way to do these things," Stambaugh said. "Go get the shotgun and a chair, Pat. Then lock that office, because that other gun is there."

Shane pitched his hat into the corner and went out whistling, but Hewitt noticed that he spurted across the line of fire without wasting time. Neither did he waste it when he returned, pushing the swivel chair on its casters and carrying the shotgun.

He placed the chair with its back to the wood-sheathed corridor wall, near the door to the corridor, but well out of the line of fire from the window.

"Here all right, Mr. Hewitt?"

"That's fine. How are you loaded?"

"One bird and one buck." Shane patted his shirt pocket. "One bird and one buck here."

"Sure you remember which barrel is loaded with which?"

Shane grinned. "I may be crazy, Mr. Detective, but I ain't *in*-tirely stupid."

"I guess not. Pat, don't just get excited and blast away, but don't get caught with your pants down, either. If he gets a chance and makes a break, try to shoot his legs out from under him. But if you have to, kill him."

Hewitt spoke in a normal tone of voice, so De Freese could hear, but it was not entirely for the prisoner's benefit. Shane had proved that he did not lack courage, but he had a clown streak that did not mix with this kind of work.

Shane nodded. He was serious enough now. Hewitt held out his hand. Stambaugh put the key in it, and Hewitt ducked quickly through the door and into the cellblock corridor.

There was no shot through the window. Hewitt put the key in the big steel padlock and clicked it open. "Come on, Pearl," he said. "We have a question or two that we'd like you to answer."

CHAPTER ELEVEN

"Sit there." Hewitt pointed to Stambaugh's bunk, with its blanket neatly tucked in over the pillow.

"Listen, there ain't nothing I can tell you, but if you want to waste your time, go ahead," De Freese said as he sat down.

"Now, take off your boots," said Hewitt.

"What?"

"Off with them! You don't need to use your hands, boy. Just kick them off and kick them over this way."

"What the hell is this?" De Freese blustered. "I ain't going to undress like that baboon in there."

Hewitt took the sap from his pocket and waggled it at De Freese. "We can argue about it all afternoon, or I can take your boots off myself—and I haven't time to argue."

One at a time, De Freese hooked his boots off with his toes.

"I said kick them across to the deputy marshal!"

De Freese gave up and kicked the boots across the room. Stambaugh picked up the right one first and found in it a stiff, double-edged knife made from an eight-inch file. The edges had been hand-forged and then ground; the handle was a wrapping of bicycle tape.

"Now let's unbutton your shirt," Hewitt said.

De Freese knew better than to argue now. He ripped the shirt open, losing two buttons doing it, and let them see the knife hanging in a sheath by a string around his neck. He took it off at a gesture from Hewitt by lifting the loop over his head. He threw it, sheath and all, on the floor in front of Hewitt.

Hewitt kicked it over to where Stambaugh could pick it up. He put the sap back in his pocket, sat down beside Stambaugh, and leaned his elbows on his knees. He took out a cigar, licked it thoughtfully, and lighted it without taking his eyes off the prisoner.

"It would take both of those knives and one more like it, Pearl, to make an even fight between us. I just don't want you hurting yourself, is all. Now, you're going to answer some questions, either before or after I work you over with the cosh. Which way do you like it?" he said.

De Freese's eyes glittered back at him. "I don't know what I can tell you, but I ain't got nothing to hide and there ain't nothing you can beat out of me."

"Fine! What part of the country do you come from, Pearl? Where were you born?"

"Wray, Colorado. I never was in no trouble there. What difference does it make?"

It gave Hewitt a feeling of confidence to have come so close to guessing De Freese's origin. "How old were you when you left there?"

"Seventeen."

"Went to New York, didn't you?"

De Freese, surprised, blinked and nodded. Hewitt went on:

"Did some fighting there, didn't you? Under what name?"

"Mickey O'Ryan."

"Ever fight in Atlantic City?"

"No."

"Philadelphia?"

"Yes."

"Buffalo?"

"Once."

"Cleveland?"

"Yes."

"Chicago?"

"Yes."

"How long were you in Cleveland?"

"All one winter."

"It's a good fight town, isn't it?"

"I don't know what the hell—"

"Just answer my question, Pearl."

"All right, it's a good fight town."

"How long were you in Chicago?"

"Listen, I made a mistake there. I never fought in Chicago. I went through there, but—"

"Cut it out, Pearl. What name did you fight under in Chicago? Do you want to tell me, or shall I tell you?"

De Freese looked down between his feet. His toes were out of both socks and were filthy. The sight seemed to embarrass him.

"Kid Callahan."

"Once more, now—how long were you there?"

"Well, let's see, I fought three fights, and—"

"How long were you there?"

"Most of a year."

"What are you wanted for there?"

"Jesus, who said I was wanted there? Hell, I can go any-place in the world I ever been, and—"

"Cut it out! You can't keep your hands off other people's money, can you? Other people too. Assault with intent to commit murder—that's what they called it, wasn't it? Let's turn our cards up, Pearl!"

"I don't know what they called it," De Freese said, "but nobody cheats me. Nobody!"

"If you're going to throw fights," Hewitt said, "that's the kind of people you do business with. When did you leave Chicago?"

(Days later, Pat Shane was to say, "What I still don't understand is how you knew all that about the way he fought for a living and where he fought." And Hewitt would say, "He's a man with a million-dollar body, a ten-cent brain, and the heart of a two-bit whore. Waterfront towns are all good fight towns. Those questions would fit anyone with a mug like his.")

De Freese struggled to remember when he left Chicago. "Just the month," Hewitt prodded him. "We don't need the day and the hour."

"Well, I forget just when it was."

"I see. Where did you go?"

"Canada. A town called Portage la Prairie."

"And where did you go from Portage la Prairie?"

"Here. I came to here from there."

"No stops along the way? Come on, Pearl!"

"Don't call me that!"

"Where were you two weeks ago today?"

A startled scowl darkened De Freese's face. "Two weeks ago today? What's that got to do with it?"

"All right, three weeks ago today. Think back."

"Hell, how do I know where I was? I came here from Portage la Prairie, goddam it! I can't keep track of where I was every goddam day, can I?"

"But this is your first time in Kaylee's Ford?"

"I told you that!"

"Tell me again, only tell the truth this time."

"I never was here before."

"Say, six weeks ago today—where were you?"

"Six weeks? Hell, still up in Canada."

Beside Hewitt on the bunk, Stambaugh said, "Wait a minute, Mr. Hewitt. Let me talk to this jaybird a minute. What were you doing for a living in Canada?"

"There was a man there, selling sheep to the settlers, fifteen thousand head. I helped him take care of his sheep."

"Let's see your hands. Stick them out. No, turn them over, palms up. Open them up!"

"What the hell is this all about?"

"You got calluses that thick, herding sheep? You never worked in a shingle mill or a lumber camp, did you? Those look like the callus marks of a crosscut saw."

De Freese jerked his hands back as though they had been burned. His right shot out again, the forefinger pointing at Stambaugh. "Looky here, the man you want shoots a Winchester rifle, like new, a Model Seventy-three with a sharpshooter's thumbhole stock. *He's* the man you want."

Stambaugh looked at Hewitt, a glance that said, Take it from here. . . . Hewitt said, "Want for what, Pearl? Now we're getting somewhere, aren't we?" De Freese clenched his jaw and looked down at his hands, slowly curling them into fists. "Where did you see this man with the Winchester Seventy-three, Pearl?" Hewitt went on. "Do you want to put a date on it? Or do you want me to?"

The outer door opened, and a man came striding through the empty outer office. Shane raised his eyebrows at Hewitt, who shook his head: No, keep your eye on the prisoner! Never relax for a second. . . .

The door opening on the corridor was thrown back, and Edwin W. Newhart-Poulton came into the room. Hewitt jumped up and held up his hand, palm outward. "Watch it! Don't come between the man with the shotgun and the prisoner. Stay back—stay back!"

Newhart-Poulton stopped just in time. "Sorry. Where are those two rock heads of mine that you had in jail here? They didn't report back to work."

"I doubt if they've left town," Hewitt said. You just bet they haven't, he thought. They've still got some money coming. . . .

Newhart-Poulton's ruddy face grew redder, but the finger he pointed at Hewitt was like a schoolteacher's, angry but rather prim. "You had your way, and I'm moving my road. I can take my caning, but I'm a poor loser. Now I have witnesses who saw those men on the street just before three-thirty in the morning! And I'm not going to be satisfied merely to jail them for dynamiting that road—with my own dynamite, incidentally. I'm going to sign a criminal complaint against you, and I'll see you go to prison for it, too, if it costs me ten thousand dollars!"

"What if it costs you twelve thousand?" Hewitt looked at Shane and said, "Pat! Go around him, and get over by the wall near your prisoner."

Pat stood up. The still room echoed suddenly to the ominous double click as he cocked both barrels. He held the gun in front of him, muzzle pointed to the ceiling. He stepped smartly past Newhart-Poulton, and Hewitt saw De Freese tense and then relax, as Shane got past Newhart-Poulton before De Freese could make his jump.

Newhart-Poulton blinked impatiently. He had a problem on his mind, and the interrogation of a dangerous prisoner was not going to come between him and the answers he demanded. He said, impatiently, "Twelve thousand? I'm afraid you're talking in riddles, Mr. Hewitt. I told you I had witnesses who—"

Hewitt cut in, "I can buy that kind of witnesses for ten dollars apiece. Forget your damned road a moment and look at that man. Have you ever seen him before? And be damned sure of your answer, because *you* could end up as a witness, yourself."

Newhart-Poulton turned and looked at De Freese— looked over and through him, rather than at him. "I may have. I see hundreds of men—thousands of them!"

Stambaugh took a step toward Newhart-Poulton. He would have taken another, except that Hewitt stopped him before he could come that close to De Freese.

"Now, goddam it to hell, but I have taken all the im-

pudence from you that I mean to take, Mr. Newhart-
Poulton," Stambaugh said, a quiver in his voice betraying
the anger he was no longer trying to hold back. "Turn
around again and look at that man. Look at him carefully!
Have you ever seen him before? Did he ever hit you up for
a job? Do you recognize him at all?"

Again Newhart-Poulton looked at De Freese. "Let me
see, let me see. Why, you're that fighter chap, that's who
you are! You wanted a job as a gun guard—yes, I recall you
now!"

"That's a goddam lie!" De Freese said.

"How dare you!" De Freese tensed again, as Newhart-
Poulton turned back to Stambaugh, but he caught Hewitt's
eye on him and sat back again. Newhart-Poulton said, "One
doesn't forget a physique like his, Mr. Deputy. I do
definitely remember him. He asked me for a guard's job.
I told him my guards and watchmen were all either picked
from my old, tested laborers, or hired through an agency. I
offered him a job breaking rock. As strong as he is, he could
have made good money. He turned it down."

Hewitt could hear Stambaugh's taut and rapid breathing.
He was having trouble controlling his own breath.

"Can you remember when that was?" Stambaugh said.
"Take your time. Try to associate it with where you were,
what you were doing at the time, what hour of the day it
was. See if you can bring back what date it was."

"I remember it clearly, now, because after he turned the
job down, I asked him if he were not a professional prize-
fighter. I've got a couple of prizefighters on my crew, and
I thought perhaps we might stage a fight to amuse the men
and perhaps give the natives a treat."

Stambaugh looked at Hewitt, who kept looking at De
Freese, as he said, "Go on, Mr. Newhart-Poulton, try to
remember the date. *Pat!* Watch him, *watch him!*"

"I think I'll chain him," Stambaugh said.

"Not now!" Hewitt said sharply. "Stay put. Nobody moves!"

Newhart-Poulton said, "It was just before noon, at my office tent. I was short of time, because I had an appointment at two-thirty with the division engineer of the railroad at the depot. I believe he could recall the date from his records, because he had the division superintendent with him, and we were in conference until—until—until—"

Newhart-Poulton gagged and turned white. His chin worked. He got it out somehow: "That was when the chap —young Patterson—was seeking help to look for his missing sister. My God, it was the day of her murder! Is this fighter chap the man you—?"

"Oh no you don't!" Pat Shane shouted.

De Freese jumped for the man with the shotgun, rather than toward liberty. He hit Shane twice, once over the heart and once under the ear. Shane clung to the shotgun, but he went down to his knees.

De Freese whirled, and Hewitt thought he was still feinting, and took time to get his .45 out. De Freese instead dived at the bunk where Hewitt and Stambaugh had been sitting. Stambaugh threw himself at him, took an elbow across his nose, and still got hold of De Freese's denim vest and hung on.

De Freese snatched up the knife that Stambaugh had left on the bunk—the short, carbon-steel, double-edged one hand-forged from an eight-inch file. He put the lump of bicycle tape that was its handle against his palm. He clenched his teeth as he drove it into Stambaugh so far that he did not even try to pull it out.

He threw Stambaugh at Hewitt and headed for the door. Stambaugh was already bleeding at the mouth, as well as in the lower chest, around the knife. Hewitt saw Pat Shane go reeling after De Freese with the shotgun. He picked himself up after lowering Stambaugh to the floor, and went after Pat with the .45 in his hand.

De Freese had untied Newhart-Poulton's little gray mare. Shane did not bother to call to him. He fired one barrel of the shotgun into the air and the mare went crazy. She went up on her hind legs and danced backward, and De Freese wept and cursed and tried to pull her down to where he could get a foot in the stirrup.

Shane fired the other barrel—the one loaded with buck-shot—from the hip, from ten or twelve feet away. The impact knocked De Freese over on his side and half tore him in two. He twitched lightly a couple of times and was dead.

Hewitt heard Shane reload the shotgun as he ran back to the bullpen cell, Shane at his heels. Newhart-Poulton was kneeling beside Stambaugh.

"Nothing anyone can do, Mr. Hewitt," he said, looking up. "Heavens, it went all the way through him—it's sticking out his back!"

Stambaugh was still alive. His eyes beseeched Hewitt, who dropped to his knees beside him. "My fault, Mr. Stambaugh," Hewitt said.

"No, mine," said Stambaugh. "I knew I should have had him in chains, but I hate chains so much! Listen, Mr. Hewitt —what you're thinking, it's all wrong. It's all wrong, all wrong."

The blood welled up in his throat, and he gagged and then went limp as his heart stopped. "The hell of it is, Mr. Stambaugh, I'm not wrong," Hewitt said softly as he stood up. He looked at Shane. "You're in charge now, Pat."

"Me? Hell, I don't know anything about this business!" Pat said brokenly. He could not tear his eyes off Stambaugh's body. "Will you stay and help finish it?"

"I'll stay, and you can bet your last dime that we'll finish it," Hewitt said.

"That fighter chap," said Newhart-Poulton. "Is he the man who murdered that little girl?"

"No, but he was a witness to something, a witness I never expected to have, and then I let him get away."

"You mean," said Shane, "you think you know who the murderer is?"

"I've been fairly sure from the first. The problem was to prove it on him."

"What do we do now, with no witness?"

"We start over again," Hewitt said.

CHAPTER TWELVE

Hewitt blamed himself. Pat Shane blamed himself. Robert E. Lee Stambaugh had died, blaming himself. Mr. Edwin W. Newhart-Poulton blamed all of them. It was the most inept police work he had ever seen.

"And you put those two rock heads up to dynamiting that road, Mr. Hewitt!" he scolded, shaking his finger in Hewitt's face. "Don't forget, we're still going to come to a settlement for that."

"You bet we are, Mr. Newhart-Poulton," Hewitt said, "and we're going to start right now. If you don't get out of here, I'm going to close your quarry down and set fire to your tents."

"You wouldn't dare try it! You couldn't get away with it if you did."

Hewitt took out his watch, the gift of a client, a rich man very like Mr. Edwin W. Newhart-Poulton. "Shall we butt heads on that?" he said. "You have ten seconds to get the hell out of the presence of a dead man who was my friend and Pat Shane's."

"How can I? You let my horse get away! I'll be damned if I—all right, all right, I'm leaving!"

He left in a furious huff, but he left. The two shotgun blasts had brought a dozen men on the run, most of them from the Battlefield Saloon. Hewitt sent one of them for Dr. Tabery.

"Who is the federal judge who commissioned you?" he asked Shane.

"Judge Anderson, in Minneapolis."

"You have his exact name and address?"

"Sure!"

"It's time to wire him to get on the job here and do his duty. Are you game?"

"You write her out, Jeff, and I'll sign her."

"How about the county judge?"

"He's staying with his brother-in-law on a cow ranch east of here. It's on the railroad. I'll wire him, too, if you like."

"I would like."

Shane was close to tears. "Lee whipped me about like I was his fetch-dog, but he was a good man."

"The best. I want to ask you something about him, Pat, that must be strictly between us. I'm sure you must have suspected that he was in love with Mrs. Johnco. He never fooled around there, did he?"

Shane said thoughtfully, "I seen the way he looked at her, and I reckon you're right. She didn't know he was alive, and the kind of a man he was—" Shane shook his head and looked down at the dead deputy marshal. "She was somebody else's wife. He would've cut off his hand before he'd've touched her."

"Way I figure it. Let's get busy on those telegrams. Send one of those saloon bums to find Mrs. Patterson, just in case she's not at the depot. These must go at the urgent rate and go immediately."

To the Hon. Almon T. C. Anderson, District Judge, United States Court House, in Minneapolis, went this wire, signed by P. J. Shane, Dep. U.S. Marshal:

BEG REPORT DEP. U.S. MARSHAL STAMBAUGH MURDERED TODAY STOP MURDERER KILLED RESISTING ARREST BY UNDERSIGNED STOP SUBMIT THAT ORDER IS RESTORED HERE LACKING ONLY JUDICIARY STOP VACUUM OF AU-

THORITY FILLABLE ONLY BY COURT OR MARTIAL LAW
STOP UNDER GOVERNING STATUTES MY NEXT RECOURSE
THE PRESIDENT STOP KINDLY ADVISE YOUR RESPECTFUL
SERVANT WHO IS MAN ON THE SPOT

To Hon. Tecumseh Fielding, County Judge, went this
telegram, also signed by Shane, in care of his brother-in-
law:

FEDERAL AUTHORITY CANNOT INTERPOSE FOREVER BE-
TWEEN YOU AND CONSTITUENCY STOP INQUEST ON FELONY
DEATH MARSHAL STAMBAUGH IMPERATIVE STOP BELIEVE
LOCAL BAR WILL ENDORSE UNDERSIGNEDS REQUEST YOU
RETURN CONDUCT SAME AND KNOW LOCAL VOTERS WILL
STOP WHEN CAN I EXPECT YOU QUESTION MARK MOST
RESPECTFULLY YOURS

"I dunno, threatening the federal judge with asking the
President for martial law, and telling the county judge
he's obligated to conduct the inquest—is that good law?"
Shane asked.

"I don't know, but I'm sure we'll soon find out. It's good
politics, at the very least," Hewitt said.

Shane leaned over the desk to scrawl his signature on
both telegrams. Before they could be handed to a man to
take to Roma Patterson at a dead run, she appeared at the
courthouse in person.

"I have a wire for you, Mr. Hewitt," she said; and no one
could have accused either of collusion, so distant was her
tone. "It's so long, I thought I would bring it in person."

He motioned to Shane to close the door to the bullpen
cell, to spare her the sight of Stambaugh's body. He took
the telegram—six pages, in her easily-read hand—and
merely glanced through them.

"I suppose there's a copy of this in the copy press," he said.

"Of course," she said; but she shook her head, almost imperceptibly.

"Thank you very much, Mrs. Patterson. You'll hear it anyway, so I'm obliged to tell you that Deputy Marshal Stambaugh was murdered a few moments ago."

"Anything to do with my daughter's death?"

"Yes." He wanted to tell her that he thought the murder that still tore at her heart was close to solution, but there were too many avid ears present. He said only, "It was his job, Mrs. Patterson. Don't regret anything. Leave everything to Pat Shane and me."

"Yes. I better get these on the wire."

She held the tears as long as she was in sight of anyone at the courthouse, anyway. Dr. Tabery arrived, a fat, wheezing man of few words. A very few of them sufficed to scatter the loafers and send them back to the saloon in considerable haste.

He knelt beside Stambaugh's body and verified what he already knew. He struggled to his feet.

"A good man," he said.

"He said the same about you," said Hewitt.

"You're Mr. Hewitt, I presume. I embalmed the body of Loretta Patterson for her father. Don't know if he is yet in shape to take care of this one. I'll need his team and hearse, though."

"Why not just tell him there's a job to do, Doctor? He impresses me as a man with the necessary guts for whatever his position obliges him to do."

"Probably." Dr. Tabery indicated the body of Stambaugh with his hand. "Too bad he did not."

"Did not what?"

"Have the necessary guts. He passed the buck to you. *He* knew that poor, stupid rock head wasn't guilty."

"But could he have proved it?"

"By arresting the guilty man—yes."

"Are you implying that—?"

"I'm not implying anything! I'm telling you that, after a couple of days, he knew—he *knew*—who the murderer was. To anticipate your next question—no, I did not discuss it with him. He carefully did not discuss it with me. Why, man, anyone with the slightest intelligence, and with the sophistication any peace officer should possess, could not help knowing the truth!"

"Who else knew it, besides you and Stambaugh?"

"No one. This is not to the discredit of people here, Mr. Hewitt. You and I know things about our fellow human beings that I, personally, wish I did not know. The price of knowledge is loss of innocence."

Hewitt looked at Shane. "Pat, go get Nate Patterson's team and the hearse. If he'll come too, ask him to do so. Then you relieve me here."

"Relieve you? Doing what?"

"Keeping our prisoner safe! Tcherin, I mean. One more death—how do we know how the people are going to react to it?"

"By God, you're keeping something back from me!"

"That's right. I can do things that you can't, because you're a federal officer. This is the way the cards fall, Pat. On the double!"

"You are sure as hell free with the orders," Shane said, without heat, as he went out.

"Have somebody bring my horse here!" Hewitt called after him.

"Yessir! Coming right up, sir."

The outer door slammed. At the other end of the corridor, Emil Tcherin kept pacing, pacing, pacing. The slither and click of the horny soles of his bare feet was the only sound in the building.

Dr. Tabery sat down heavily on the bunk Stambaugh had used. "Exactly what happened? How was he killed? I presume that dead one outside is part of it. No need to stop and feel of his pulse, I assure you."

Hewitt told him of his arrest of Pearl De Freese, and the interrogation that had gone wrong when Mr. Edwin W. Newhart-Poulton insisted on giving priority to his own problems.

"I should have questioned him in the cell, or chained him, but it was Stambaugh's jail."

"And Stambaugh's hopeless illusion. I'm sure that you, with your background, knew better."

"I knew who was the logical candidate. Proving it was a rooster with a different kind of tail."

"Can you prove it now?"

"I mean to be in that position soon."

"Poor Stambaugh! So tough, so fearless, in so many ways —so weak and innocent in others."

"It's the penalty of self-education, Doctor. I came that path myself. Acquiring knowledge is a much swifter business than learning to have confidence in yourself as an educated man."

"I don't imagine you ever lack confidence."

"I have my private moments of self-doubt," Hewitt said, "but they never weaken me. When I lack cocksureness, I pretend to be cocksure. That's almost as good."

"I know what you mean! Wait until you have to cut into a man on the basis of your own hasty diagnosis," Dr. Tabery said. "I've been pretending cocksureness for nearly thirty-six years now. The load never gets any lighter."

"I can believe that."

"I wouldn't trade places with you today. You are going to make your move this afternoon, aren't you?"

"As soon as Pat gets back."

"I don't envy you, sir, indeed I don't."

"It'll be easy, Doctor," Hewitt said softly.

Rowdy was upset, Rowdy felt neglected and wanted to run. Hewitt kept him dancing at a slow pace until he was sure the storm inside himself had subsided. He put Robert E. Lee Stambaugh out of his mind entirely and saw to it that this was just another job of work.

It was the hottest afternoon yet in Kaylee's Ford. He passed the meat market, where two stray cowboys, one a luckless, chinless, and almost witless drifter, the other a killer waiting to kill or be killed, had tried to waylay Mrs. Johnco. He passed the spot where he had dropped both of them, and wished he could go back to that moment and make it possible for Lee Stambaugh to live.

Blue-green dragonflies slashed through the sunlight, and when he passed under the trees as he neared the Johnco place, he heard both the *kak-kak-kak-kak-kak* of a locust and the smart-aleck barking of a red squirrel. He had never smelled green trees more sharply, never felt the difference between sun-heat and shade-cool as keenly, never seen color as vividly.

He tied Rowdy securely to a limb of a tree and walked the last dozen or so feet. He knocked sharply on the door, waited, and then knocked again.

"I'm out back!" came Mrs. Johnco's voice.

He took it as an invitation and opened the door and went in. He closed the door behind him and saw the chair and the couch, and Johnco's bedclothes stacked neatly at the end of the couch, and the pictures leaning against the wall. He went on into the tiny kitchen where she had made tea and sandwiches and took a quick look around without stopping.

He opened the back door and stepped out into a tiny

yard where the grass grew almost ankle deep, and the surrounding trees were a background of beauty that whispered with every breeze. Mrs. Johnco was sitting in a creaking old home-made chair, the lumber for which had come from some yellow-painted shack.

"Oh! I thought it was my husband," she said. She did not look particularly startled—surprised, perhaps, but not unpleasantly so.

"Sorry, ma'am. He's the one I wanted to see," Hewitt said, taking his hat off with his left hand. "I thought maybe I'd catch him painting. Where does he work?"

"Here." She did not get up, but gestured with both hands. "He has no studio, naturally, in so small a house. But when there's light here, he says, this is the grandest light of all for a painter."

"I can see that. There used to be some flowers behind you there, I'll bet."

"Yes, how did you know?"

"There are flowers behind you in that picture."

"Oh yes." Her color rose a little, but she was not offended. "It's as private here as a studio would be. If—if I may guess what you're thinking Mr. Hewitt—yes, I have posed for him here."

"That's what I was thinking, ma'am."

"That surely isn't what you wanted to discuss with my husband, though."

"No, ma'am. I wanted to see his rifle."

"He hasn't got a rifle," she said quickly.

"I think he has. He's an ace sharpshooter, and he's got a Winchester Model Seventy-three with a target stock, with a thumbhole."

"Oh, you're mistaken!"

"I'm not mistaken, Mrs. Johnco, and I never have been —not for one God-blasted, accursed minute."

Her hands dropped to her lap and closed tightly, one on

each magnificent upper leg. She had started to turn pink, until he said "rifle." She had paled just a little then, but she went ashen now.

"Mr. Hewitt," she said, "take me away from here with you."

"Where to?" he said.

"Anywhere. Now! The evening train east. God, Mr. Hewitt, have pity on me, have mercy! I—I'm hungry. I—I haven't had enough to eat lately. He—we're out of money and there's nothing left to sell. Oh God, get me out of here, please, Mr. Hewitt!"

"How can you be going hungry? You've been getting checks for—"

"Those? Oh, not for months—not for months! I sold some jewelry and sent the money to a friend in France, and she sent me forty dollars a month while it lasted. I'm past shame. That's what hunger does to you, Mr. Hewitt. Adrian got a deer, a small fawn rather, a month ago. We ate that until it was gone. I spent our last twelve cents on veal—twelve cents, do you hear? I had to ask him to cut it in two because it was twenty cents. That's why I was so rude to you—*because I didn't have the other eight cents!*"

She was not a woman to weep, and she held back the tears now, but it was a narrow thing. Hewitt said, "But ma'am, if your husband hasn't got a rifle, how did he get a deer? Run it down and choke it to death with his bare hands? You know why I want him."

Her eyes met his, and locked. "You think he killed the Patterson girl."

"I know he killed the Patterson girl."

"No—no—*no!* Just because he's different—because he's a painter and musician—"

"He's different, all right. There's no reward on this case. The Pattersons are poor folks. I'll make you a deal, though. I'll collect the reward on you and hand you a thousand dollars of it when I've got it in hand, if you'll come down to the courthouse and surrender."

The look she gave him now had no pretense, no bluff in it. "You've got your guts, Mr. Hewitt. What good is a thousand dollars going to do me in jail?"

"You can handle that, all right. The warrant's only a technicality, and you damn well know it. All he wants is to get you back. You twisted him around your finger before. Can't you do it again?"

"Mr. Hewitt, if I go back to Chicago, it will be in handcuffs. You can't prove anything on Adrian."

"Come in the house. Let me show you something, show you how boringly stupid it is of you to argue."

He opened the back door and held it open, and she could no more resist that challenge than she could any. She went in ahead of him. He let the door close and started going through the things in the kitchen. She watched him empty cans and turn drawers upside down and feel on empty top shelves. There was not so much as a raw bean to be cooked.

"Where are your husband's paints?" he asked, and he hoped she could not guess how thin this cocksureness was.

"Oh, you'll enjoy this! It used to be the woodshed. In the winter, it still is the woodshed, but it's the only place a wonderfully talented artist has to store the few things he still has left. He's all out of paint, Mr. Hewitt. All out! Even a dabbler should know what it's like for a painter out of paints."

She threw back the door to a windowless lean-to, no more than eight feet square. It was empty except for the bark and trash from firewood, and the mice who lived and bred and lived out their lives in it, innocent of complicity in the lives of the deomorphic bipeds who shared the house with them. Johnco's palette, his brushes in their tall jars of turpentine, and his tubes squeezed dry of paint, were on a wooden bench along one wall.

There was also a tall pottery jar with a lid on it. Hewitt picked it up, turned it on its side, and let the lid fall to the ground. He poured a handful of big, brightly colored jelly beans out into his palm.

"Where did these come from?" he said.

"Oh my God, I forgot all about them, and I'll bet he did too, or they'd have been eaten long ago!" she cried.

He let her take a handful and put them in her mouth, but he picked the lid up off the ground and put it on the jar to save the rest.

"Know where they came from, Mrs. Johnco?"

"I think from a town in Nebraska—it's called Valentine, I believe. He bought them, all the store had, when we came through there. He likes something sweet to nibble on when he paints. What difference does it make where he got them?"

"A lot of these were found on the body of the Patterson girl, and her stomach was full of them," Hewitt said.

"Oh, my God, no, no, no!"

Suddenly she threw up the jelly beans she had swallowed. She groped blindly for the door to the kitchen. He caught both arms from behind to steady her. After a few steps, she was able to shake his hands off and walk, falteringly, without his aid. She did not stop until she was in the center of the living room.

She put her palms to her cheeks and closed her eyes. "Oh no, it's a nightmare. It isn't true!"

"It's true, and you've known it in your heart for quite a while, haven't you? You've made him sleep on the couch —for how long? You may not know what he's been shooting at, but you can't help knowing he has been slipping up to the top of the hill and firing at something. You let him take food to Emil Tcherin—food you needed to keep from starving to death!—and you couldn't help knowing why. Not out of the goodness of his heart, because he's a mean, petty, bullying tyrant of a man, isn't he? But because sticking up for Tcherin was the surest way in the world to deflect suspicion from himself!"

She opened her eyes and stared into his. "You must be sure. You wouldn't say this unless you knew, would you? Oh God, I never really suspected—I couldn't let myself—I never faced it—but you're sure?"

"I'm sure. I had a witness for a while too. He saw something, anyway. Saw your husband, well enough to identify his rifle."

He went over and put his hand on her upper arm to steady her. "I'm sorry for you. You've made the most of your troubles, but you weren't asking for this. It's too bad you have to be caught in it."

"Take me with you away from here, Mr. Hewitt. I beg you—I'll get down on my knees—I'll do anything—I'll see that you're never sorry."

"You know I can't."

"You can, you know you can! Just give me money for a ticket—oh God, just to the next town, even—before you let anybody know. I—can't face—I can never—I'll make you happy, I promise I will."

"I can't, and the hell of it is, I don't even want to. Mrs. Johnco—"

"That's not my name. That was my maiden name."

"Merle, then. You're such a goddam liar that you even lied to yourself about a little girl's murder. What kind of idiot would I be to believe anything you say?"

"Merle!" came a voice from outside. "Are you here, Merle? I've torn my hand. Merle, my God, you know how I am about blood! Bring a cloth, Merle, please!"

"It's Adrian, and he's got the rifle with him," she whispered through chattering teeth.

"Yes," Hewitt said, "and I know how he is about blood too."

CHAPTER THIRTEEN

She clutched at his arm, as he slid toward the front door. "Go on out and take care of his hand," he whispered. "I'll come around the house. All you have to do is stay out of the way."

"You're not going to kill him are you?" she said too loudly.

"Sh-h! I'm going to try not to. I'm going to try not to let him kill me, either."

"I can't face him."

"You have to. If I go out that back door, it's him or me, you know that."

"I'm not going. I can't face him."

He jerked his arm loose from her clinging hands and took her wrist roughly in his. He forced her back by twisting her arm and said between his teeth, "You've been facing him, and you don't know any more now than you have all along."

"You'll kill him."

"By God, I will if you make me! It's up to you."

He wondered how much of her terror was assumed, how much real. He could not believe she was really afraid of Johnco—or for that matter, of any man alive. He opened the front door quietly and slipped out. Before closing it, he saw her start back through the kitchen. Her walk was as steady, and as swayingly, opulently provocative, as ever.

Rowdy shot his ears at Hewitt, and Hewitt came to a stop in the shade of a tree that brushed the house, frowning, trying to remember how it was behind the house. Could Johnco have come from the rear, from the timber somewhere, and not seen the horse? Could he have come down from the bald hilltop without seeing it?

Certainly not the latter. No, he knew Hewitt was here, he had probably been listening to Hewitt and the woman for God knew how long. That whimpering wail about tearing his hand was a bit of stagecraft. He was back there with his rifle, a wanted man who knew he was wanted—and wanted for hanging.

Nothing to do but go after him, but first, Hewitt had to decide which way to go around the house. There was not much cover to the south, if he remembered accurately from climbing the hill with Stambaugh. It might not be any better on the other side, but it could be no worse.

He heard voices and down the path came Toby Parmenter and Mac MacAdams, lounging along and quarreling in their usual amiable way. He ran out far enough to make sure they saw him, and shook his head and waved a signal to come on—hurry—and be quiet!

They could take orders. They broke into a silent tiptoe run and both made sure of their guns. He pulled their heads close to his and whispered, "Boys, there's a man out back with a Winchester, and I've got to take him alive. You go around the outside, one each way. I'll go back through the house. Let's watch our chance and pile on him."

"The son of a bitch that killed that little girl?" Toby said.

"That's my man."

"Why do you care whether he's killed or not?"

"I've still got to prove it on him, and he's due for a good hanging. Do it my way or git."

Yes, they could take orders. They split, Mac taking the north side of the house, Toby the south. Hewitt let himself back inside and went softly through the house. The floor creaked, but not loudly, and he was keyed up to where he was sure what was in Johnco's mind. Johnco was sly, not brilliant or daring. Johnco would have heard him say he was going around the house, and Hewitt would disappoint him if he did anything else.

He saw them clearly, standing in the center of the pretty little grassy glade that was where Johnco painted. He had the rifle muzzle touching the woman's stomach, with her back to the kitchen door, Johnco facing it.

"I don't care if you do," the woman was saying.

"Please don't treat me like a fool, Merle," said Johnco. "You wouldn't trade your life for anyone's, least of all a common detective's."

"That's how little you know me, Adrian."

Johnco jiggled the rifle against her, for emphasis. "I know you better than you know yourself, my dear. I've turned you inside out a thousand times. You're a selfish, nasty, willful, thieving child, and a liar besides."

"No, really you don't know me," she said sedately, "honestly you don't, if you think I'm afraid to die since I know you killed that little girl."

He smiled and shook his head. "Call him. You may as well call him. You're not convincing me at all."

"And you can't scare me any more, you miserable, impotent rapist."

"Ah, that's where you're wrong, dear. You should have been nicer to me. None of this would have happened."

"It's my fault you killed her, that's what you mean."

"It would not have happened if you had been a woman instead of a street cur in heat."

Well, I've heard enough, Hewitt thought. That's as close as he's going to come to admitting it, without killing her. . . . He put both hands on the screen door, in plain sight, and pushed it open slightly.

"Hold your fire, Johnco," he called, not loudly, because

if he startled Johnco, he had only to clench his hands and the rifle would fire. "I'm coming out. Let's make a deal."

Hewitt knew how close the woman had come to death, whether she did or not. Johnco kept the gun against her while he risked looking over her head at Hewitt in the doorway. Hewitt stepped outside, keeping both hands elevated.

The door slammed shut behind him. Johnco smiled. "That's good sense, Mr. Hewitt," he said. "Keep those hands up where I can see them and come toward me. There, that's far enough."

Hewitt had taken three steps before Johnco stopped him. Johnco stepped back two paces himself. He waved the rifle barrel at the woman.

"Back there beside him, so I can watch you both. Now, what do you call a deal, Mr. Hewitt?"

The woman stopped beside Hewitt, so close that their arms touched, and he had the strange sensation that she was his, and as brave as she had to be, and that they would come out of this together or die together. She had the makings of that kind of woman in her . . . or had had, once.

"How about a ten-minute head start?" Hewitt said.

"Afoot? You smart son of a bitch!"

The woman saw them first, and went so rigid that he could feel her arm tense against his. He saw them too, then, and said soothingly, "Take it easy, Mrs. Johnco. I've been in these circumstances before. We'll work it out."

He was sure that Toby and Mac were old veterans of the wars against the Apaches, for only from them could they have learned this kind of combat. They moved fast, but almost silently. Three steps, and they closed. Mac dived for Johnco's legs and knocked them out from under him. Toby knocked the rifle up, so that it went off harmlessly at the sky.

Toby easily wrenched the rifle out of Johnco's hand. Johnco hit the ground hard. He kicked at Mac's face with the flat heel of his handsome boot. Toby stamped—hard —on Johnco's right hand with the heel of his own boot, and held it there. His weight pinned the hand to the ground.

"Don't kill him," the woman whispered. "Oh please, don't kill him!"

"Don't worry," Hewitt told her. He walked over and stirred Johnco with his toe. "Let him up, boys. I want to search him to the bare hide, and then I want his hands tied behind him. Can you walk him down to the courthouse and deliver him to Shane?"

"You don't need to tie his hands for that," Mac said.

"We're not going to make that mistake again. If anyone wants to stop and talk or ask questions, nothing doing! Keep him moving, get him locked up in the front cell, and tell Pat to sit tight until I get there."

"The front cell? Is that the one where we was? How about if that sharpshooter cuts loose."

"He won't. This is the sharpshooter." He looked down at Johnco. "Come on, get up. Try to act like a man."

Johnco lay on the grass, sucking at the hand Toby had stamped on and staring at the sky. He sucked noisily, like a baby with a rag sugar-tit, and he smiled the blank, blithe smile of a harmless baby.

Hewitt stirred him with his toe again, a little sharply this time. "Come on, get up! You're not very good at that, and the Rule of M'Naghten won't help you."

Johnco lumbered to his feet. A long, leather bootlace from inside the house sufficed to tie his hands behind him. It seemed to Hewitt that Johnco might be starting to realize that it was not all a nightmare—that from here, all steps led to the same blind ending.

Toby and Mac let him walk between them, with what dignity he could muster, as they left the front door and headed for the courthouse and the end. The woman had turned her back when Johnco left, as though to avoid any kind of farewell. She came closer to Hewitt.

"What's the Rule of M'Naghten?" she said.

"An 1843 British decision that our courts are applying to capital cases."

"To what? What does it mean?"

"It applies to an insanity defense, in murder trials. Can he tell the difference between right and wrong?"

"Of course."

"Then he can't beat the gallows on insanity."

She crumpled a little, and again put her hands to her head in what seemed to be a characteristic attitude of frustration. "What now?" she whispered. "What am I to do?"

"Pack a suitcase."

"For—for what?"

"You're going to jail. I told you that."

"You can't be serious!" When he said nothing, she flushed angrily and raced on, "I won't be jailed. I won't be seen on the streets after he has walked there tied. I will not be shamed that way—I will not!"

"Pack a suitcase, lady, or live the next couple of weeks in what you've got on. And you will walk to the courthouse, or you will go there with your hands and feet tied—your feet, too, ma'am!—crosswise of my horse."

Hewitt felt fairly sure that Pat Shane would be a good peace officer in time. There was much he did not know, but he was not too proud to learn. They sat in the little office and talked with the door closed, after the woman had been locked in the big bullpen cell.

"How the *hell* are we going to keep a female prisoner, Jeff?"

"You've got to hire a matron. Your commission gives you the authority in an emergency, and the judge will approve it. If you don't know a woman for the job, how about Myra Green?"

"The old catamount in the restaurant? Jesus!"

"She'll be a good one. I'm going to have to stick around, Pat, until you're out of the woods here. We'll hot-bed your room, and stand watch here nights off and on."

"What does that mean?"

"We'll take turns spending the night here on duty. The man off-duty sleeps in your room."

"Good enough. What about Tcherin?"

"Wait a few days. If a judge gets here, let him handle it. The best way, somebody would file a writ of habeas corpus, and we can't respond so the judge dismisses all charges and turns him loose. The county attorney will file a criminal information on Johnco—that, by the way, is not his real name—and the judge will hold him to answer and refuse bail."

"What'll he do about the woman?"

"I hope that problem settles itself before a judge has to. There's supposed to be a telegraphic felony warrant on the way for her."

It arrived thirty minutes later, carried by a calm and grateful Roma Patterson. She and Hewitt shook hands and did not exchange a word. "What's she wanted for?" Shane said, scowling at the warrant after Mrs. Patterson had gone. "Title so-and-so—section such-and-such—that don't mean nothing to me."

Hewitt handed him the long wire from Asa Wisner:

I WILL DEDUCT TEN PER CENT REWARD IN ADVANCE IF YOU HAVE LOCATED PARTIES AS IT APPEARS STOP YOUR SUBJECT ONE RESEMBLES RANDOLPH ADRIAN JOHNSON REPEAT JOHNSON NOT JOHNCO CHOIR DIRECTOR CHORUS AND VOICE TEACHER UNSUCCESSFUL ARTIST WANTED CINCINNATI CHILD MOLESTING WANTED ROCK ISLAND CARNAL ASSAULT AND ESCAPE HAS USED ALIASES JOHANNES ADRIAN ALSO THEO RANDOLFUS ALSO DR AUGUSTE RICARDE ALSO

DR JOHANNES WAGNER STOP APPEARS IS FORMER MEDICAL STUDENT NO REWARD STOP YOUR SUBJECT TWO RESEMBLES DAUGHTER BORN THIRTY YEARS TO STANISLAUS JANKO LATER JOHNCO SOLE OWNER VLADNO BREWERY HERE STOP MAIDEN NAME MERLE ANNA JANKO OR JOHNCO TAKE YOUR PICK STOP CASE OF TOO MUCH MONEY NO MOTHER STOP SEVENTEEN ELOPED PARIS WITH MORTIMER DUDLEY ACTOR STOP BACK AT TWENTY STOP MARRIED HARRISON ADLER TWENTY TWO DIVORCED TWENTY SIX MARRIED NEIL SHIPPEY NO DIVORCE YET STOP ALL LUGGAGE MARKED MAIDEN INITIALS THUS SUSPECT BOTH SUBJECTS USED MAIDEN NAME TO CONFORM STOP SHIPPEY EXECUTOR TWO MILLION ESTATE STOP MERLE ACCUSED LOOTING SAME STOP OWN HUSBAND OFFERS TEN THOUSAND REWARD WILL SUPPLY TELEGRAPHIC FELONY WARRANT IF YOU HAVE PARTIES STOP I AM RETAINED TO FIND SAME STOP SETTLE FOR TEN PER CENT ADVANCE STOP SHIPPEY WILL LEAVE ON RECEIPT YOUR WIRE CONFIRMING STOP PLS ANS MOST URGENT

"The girl I always dreamed of," Shane grunted, handing the wire back.

"Watch her, Pat! She—she is most attractive, when she makes up her mind to try. Don't let her make a fool of you," Hewitt said.

"It might be worth the trouble, Jeff, except for one thing. Old fat Tennessee country boy ain't going to meet a woman like this every day. But I ain't going to see a friend like Lee Stambaugh stabbed to death every day, either."

"Just keep that in mind," Hewitt said.

Tcherin, on whom the world outside his cell made no impression, continued to shuffle back and forth with his head down. Keeping him until a court ordered his release was more than a formality. It would take time for people to get used to the idea of his innocence, without the drama of a habeas corpus hearing. To turn him free now might get him speedily lynched on the street.

Johnco (or whatever his name was) had the cell next to Tcherin's. That left only the big bullpen cell for the woman. Shane watched her, while Hewitt searched the cell and removed his clothing and Stambaugh's. She seemed still stunned by events, especially the strain of the long walk from her house, with Hewitt leading his horse beside them.

They closed the cell door on her at last. It seemed to break some sort of spell for her. "Where," she said, "are the personal facilities? Or do you understand what I mean, Mr. Hewitt? Must I put it in your vernacular?"

"You mean the can, ma'am," he said. "There are only chamber pots. You're going to have a woman warder. If you have any more questions, take them up with her."

She came to the barred door, her nostrils flaring in anger, her eyes glittering. "I'm going to enjoy having the last laugh on you so very much!" she said.

"Yes, ma'am," he said. "I'm going to find a woman now to take care of you. Anything else I can get for you?"

She did not bother to answer. He checked the other prisoners—Tcherin, shuffling back and forth across his cell, Johnco or whatever his name was, huddled on his side on the floor with his knees drawn up under his chin. In the little office, Shane was going through the books and papers Stambaugh had left behind.

"You know what I'm going to do, Jeff, when I'm relieved on this case?" he said. "Take a long, hot bath with yellow, homemade soap and a stiff brush. Only way I'll ever get this dirty feeling off'n me."

"You'll never get it off," Hewitt said. "You're in that kind of business, Pat."

CHAPTER FOURTEEN

For five days straight, Hewitt had met the evening train from the east; now, on the sixth, it was late. People did not know what they were expecting—a judge, for one thing, but which one? Never less than twenty or thirty people found reason to be at the depot, and there were at least that many tonight.

Toby and Mac came plodding doggedly down the tracks from town. Hewitt had heard they had been on a drunk, and they looked it. They were sober now, because one more drink would have killed them. They marched up to where Hewitt sat on the baggage truck, apart from the crowd.

"Mr. Hewitt, when you going to give me back my horse?" said Toby.

It was obviously a rehearsed speech. Hewitt said, "My horse. I won him fair and square."

"You did not! I took you for an officer, and so did Mac. So did everybody in town. And the minute you win my horse and saddle off'n me, you bragged it around that you was only a corporal. That's cheating, goddam it!"

One more thing cleared up. The two had thought he was a provost marshal's officer on their trail. They had conspired to lose Rowdy to him as a bribe; and when he had not arrested them afterward, they thought he had taken the deal.

You couldn't argue with that mentality. Myths were more important to people than the truth, every time, and the lowly enlisted man had little enough to live for. Hewitt knew, never having been more than a corporal.

"I had some cash in that pot, Toby. A hundred and twenty-five dollars, more or less," he said.

"That wouldn't've been more than a twenty-dollar pot, if I hadn't took you for a goddam officer. What kind of an ignorant poker player do you think I am?"

"I still don't feel I owe you more than a hundred and twenty-five. Will you settle for that?"

"No, sir! I want that horse."

Why? Beyond doubt, to sell to Mr. Edwin W. Newhart-Poulton, who by now could not have helped hearing about the disputed ownership of Rowdy. Everybody in town knew the story.

"Have you boys ever heard of a Captain Maxfield Auffenhaus?"

"Dutch Auffenhaus? Sure," Mac said. "A goddam West Pointer. Only he ain't a captain no more."

"Whatever he is, suppose he interceded for you, and got you back with only thirty days in the guard house, would you go? No loss of pay or rights, retention of rank, and no more than thirty days. It would solve all your problems. The Army needs you boys, and you need the Army."

They looked pathetically wistful, and Toby said, "Yes, but Dutch Auffenhaus is a colonel now. He commands Fort Kearney, and hell, you can get thirty days just for your saber not glittering!"

He could not tell them why Captain (now Colonel) Auffenhaus would be glad to do him a favor, but he felt sure that such was the case. "If I wire him, and get a wire back saying you can return on those terms, will you settle for a hundred and a quarter? Twenty-five payable now, of course—the rest when you're back in Fort Kearney."

Again that pitiful exchange of looks. "Is that the best you can do, Mr. Hewitt?" said Mac.

"The absolute best."

Both men mopped their hard yet childlike faces. "All right," Toby said. "That's not so bad, I reckon. It'll be good to see old Kearney again! When do we get the money?"

"After I hear from the colonel."

"When you going to wire him?"

"Now."

They followed him into the depot, Hewitt wondering if perhaps his luck had not changed. It was extraordinary, that Max Auffenhaus should turn out to be the CO at the very post from which the two had deserted—although come to think of it, this was a small Army, and almost anyone might be tempted to desert the fort that Max ran. He sent off the telegram at "urgent" rates, immediately:

MAXFIELD O. AUFFENHAUS COL USA

FT KEARNEY NEBRASKA REPLY PREPAID

CAN RETURN SGTS PARMENTER AND MACADAMS TO DUTY IF NO MORE THAN THIRTY DAYS NO LOSS PAY OR RANK STOP BELIEVE THEM BOTH SOLDIERS OF CHARACTER AND PATRIOTISM STOP HOW ARE YOU MAXI PAL STOP YOU WERE RIGHT IT WAS ZINFANDEL NOT CHIANTI STOP IF YOU KNEW AS MUCH ABOUT ARMY AS CALIFORNIA WINES YOU WOULD BE GENERAL AFFECTIONATELY

J HEWITT CPL USA RETD

The train—ten empty gondolas to haul rock, one box car, eight empty cattle cars, and one combined passenger, mail, and express car, pulled in as he paid for the wire, and two men got out. Hewitt was hoping for both Judge Tecumseh Fielding and Neil Shippey, and it did indeed appear that his luck had changed.

The tall, chopfallen man with the long, curly brown hair and romantic eyes—the eyes of a wounded deer—

would be a cinch to fall victim to Merle whatever-her-name-was, and he was about the right age—forty. Old enough to know better, yet never would. A born loser who did not need aces back-to-back to go mad. In the moonlight, treys back to back would look like an empire.

The other man was tall, corpulent, seedily clad in rusty serge and Congress gaiters, with the flat black hat of a country judge or a retired bishop on his sparse and stringy white hair. Such a man, Hewitt thought, could hand down a death sentence or a foreclosure decision without a qualm and dine heartily afterward—if someone else paid.

Tactfully, he looked at neither, but rather halfway between them. "Is Mr. Neil Shippey here? I'm waiting to meet Mr. Shippey."

The tall, white-haired man in gaiters came bouncing toward him, frosty blue eyes thawing, hand outstretched. "You're Mr. Hewitt? So nice to see you, so good of you to wire me! You have my wife in custody? Take me to her," he babbled.

Hewitt made the necessary lightning mental about-face, excused himself, and went over to the man with the mournful eyes. "Judge Fielding?" he said.

The eyes twinkled distantly. "Yes, and I take it that you're Deputy Marshal Hewitt."

"*Acting* deputy marshal only, Judge. I can't say how glad we all are that you're here. There's an innocent man in jail, long overdue for—"

Judge Tecumseh Fielding cut in gently, "If he's innocent, that will be established in open court. That's why we have judges in America. Of which I am one!"

"To be sure. We also have two prisoners, one on a telegraphic warrant and one on evidence, and we need—"

Again the judge interrupted him, without losing the twinkle in his eye. "You need a lesson in judicial propriety, that's what you need. If your prisoners merit incarceration, no doubt you can so show in open court. If you have been caught with your pants down, it is in open court that your butt will become embarrassingly visible."

This judge would do! Hewitt said gravely, "Yes, Your Honor. I assume court will sit tomorrow morning?"

"Yes." The judge picked up his valise. "Good night, Mr. Hewitt. I am most happy that order has been restored here."

Hewitt bowed, tactfully said nothing, and when the judge had turned away, returned to Shippey. He needed the interlude, to decide what kind of problem he had in this infatuated old fool of a husband. Shippey was almost dancing with impatience. It was easy to see that he had deluded himself into believing that, now that his wife was in jail, they would bargain on his terms.

"Where is she? Where is my wife? Sorry I couldn't get away sooner, but I had some pressing affairs to take care of first, very pressing! Where is my wife?" Shippey said in a nervous, piping voice.

"In jail. Where did you think?" said Hewitt.

"In jail? Horrible, horrible! The poor girl, couldn't you tell she was a gentlewoman?"

"Yes, but she couldn't."

"Come now, Mr. Hewitt, no levity, please! Let's get her out, get her a room in a good hotel, and—"

"Hold everything, Mr. Shippey! There's no hotel in town, good or otherwise. And this woman is being held on a felony warrant, on a complaint that you, yourself, signed. Lastly—and I have some decent hesitation in bringing this up, naturally—there's the small matter of a reward, payable now—on the spot—*this* spot, or no deal."

Mr. Shippey almost danced again, in his impatience. "I have a draft—"

"It's supposed to be a certified check."

"Very well, a certified check, it's payable to Bankers'

Bonding & Indemnity Company of Cheyenne. I cannot—"

"It will be delivered to that company."

Shippey took a fat wallet from the breast pocket of his ancient, Mother Hubbard coat, and from it extracted a certified check for nine thousand dollars, or ten thousand, less Asa's 10 per cent. Not that Hewitt had expected anything less. Asa Wisner knew how B.B. & I. did business.

Hewitt carried the old fool's suitcase to the courthouse. Pat Shane was sitting with his feet on the desk in the small office, studying a grammar that had belonged to Stambaugh. He pushed his hat back and looked over the top of the book at Hewitt.

"Judge get in?" he said.

"Yes," said Hewitt, "and so did this."

"This what?"

"This husband of our prisoner."

Shane looked at Shippey, dropped the book, and buried his face in his arms on the desk top. His huge shoulders shook with silent sobs. Hewitt managed not to smile, as he conducted Shippey into the corridor where Myra Green, sitting on a wooden chair with her feet up against the bars of the bullpen cell, was rolling a cigarette.

"This is the jail matron, Mrs. Green," said Hewitt. "Myra, this is our prisoner's husband."

Myra finished rolling her cigarette. She extended her hand to Shippey without getting up. "Nice to meet you, Mr. Shippey. I have to say this for your wife, she ain't a complainer, and that's more than you can say for her sweetie across the way," she said. She raised her voice: "Merle, honey, here's your man. Maybe you'd like him to have supper with you, through the bars? He can set here in the hall, dearie, perfectly comfortable."

"I'll be a moment," came the woman's voice, from behind the blanket that had been stretched across the corner, to give her privacy.

"Supper? Supper?" said Shippey. "What will she be served for supper?"

"Tonight it's hamhocks and beans," said Myra.

"My God! She can't eat that."

"Honey, she loves hamhocks and beans."

Shippey's eyes glittered angrily at Hewitt. "I want this woman, this lady rather, given decent food. I insist upon it. I mean to share her meals myself, to make sure what she gets."

Hewitt said, "It won't be what you're used to, but she can have anything that can be bought here in town, if you want to pay for it. You can eat with her, but you'll be out here, and she'll be in there."

The woman came out from behind the blanket. She had bathed today in the room behind the small office, with Myra in the office and Hewitt and Shane standing guard in the outer office. She had put on the same chaste, white waist with the high collar, and had taken some pains with her hair. And it was beautiful hair, truly her crowning glory, Hewitt thought.

"You shouldn't have come, Neil," she said. "I'm better off here, and really, it's not so bad."

"Merle, my dear—oh my darling," he choked. He put both hands through the bars, and she took one of them in a light, brief shake. "It'll be all right, Merle. I'm sorry I had to do this. The warrant, I mean."

"I'm sorry, too," she said. "I'm always sorry when it's too late."

"Too late?"

She came to the bars and nodded across the corridor, where Randolph Adrian Johnson, alias (among other things) Johnco, sat in a stupor in the corner.

"That? You mean Johnson?" Shippey cried. "But Merle, my dear, you're not to blame for that. He lied to you—bewitched you—took advantage of you—!"

There were tears in her eyes as she looked at Hewitt. "Get him out of here, can't you, please?" she said. "Why should he suffer for me?"

"He wants to," said Hewitt.

"They all do," she said, and declined to shame herself by wiping away the tears.

"I didn't, ma'am," Hewitt said. "Come along, Mr. Shippey. She wants to be alone."

On the morning of September 1, Hewitt slept so deeply and late that, when he finally did wake up, he lay there for several minutes before he could remember where he was. It was a hotel room in Grand Island, Nebraska—a good room, with a featherbed and a carpeted floor and a private bath. And when he looked at his watch, and saw that it was ten-twenty, he realized that he had slept thirteen hours without turning over.

Someone was knocking on the door—had been knocking for some time, he realized. He threw back the blanket and sat up, putting his feet on the floor. He was so tired and stiff, he almost cried out in pain.

"Yes?" he called. "Who is it? Just a minute!"

There was no answer. Whoever it was, had given up and gone away. Hewitt got up, staggered to the dresser, and looked at himself in the mirror. He needed a shave, first, and then a shot of bourbon whiskey, a one-pound steak with fried potatoes and two fried eggs, and at least a quart of strong, black coffee.

But instead of going after them, he sat down on the edge of the bed again, and half dozed off. I need a long, long rest, he thought. . . .

But where? The thought of city lights, music, dining, beautiful women and fine wines, repelled him. I know, by George, he thought. I'll get a job for a while, punching cows around here somewhere. Work hard, get tired, do simple things, and sleep well because I'll have only simple thoughts. . . .

That last morning in Kaylee's Ford, when the two (count them, two!) members of the Kaylee's Ford bar came out of retirement, and shared between them the wealth of clients.

Emil Tcherin, dismissed. Hewitt personally took him to the barber shop and got him a haircut and shave. He personally took him to Mr. Edwin W. Newhart-Poulton and got him his job back.

Randolph Adrian Johnson, held to answer to the crime of murder in the first degree, trial set for the third Monday in August. And then, on motion of counsel, a change of venue granted because an impartial jury could not possibly be found here.

Merle Janko, aka Johnco, aka Shippey, released on bond of ten thousand dollars in the custody of her husband.

Next, a writ of mandamus, directing the Board of County Commissioners to hold an election to fill the office of sheriff, said election to be conducted not less than sixty days nor more than ninety days from the date of said writ.

"I've got a durn good notion to stay here and run for it myself," Pat Shane said. "I kinda like this town, Jeff. Or I will when the quarry's gone."

"Nobody can beat you in an election, and you'll be a good man for the job," said Hewitt.

"That's all I wanted to hear. Soon as I can, I'm going to figger up all the bills I got to turn in, for expenses and your salary and so forth—"

"I'm waiving my salary, Pat. I don't want to—"

"Oh no you don't! You're on the federal warrant for *per diem*, and I can't get you off without'n your signature. You ain't tangling *me* up in no federal red tape like that."

Merle asked for a moment alone with Hewitt; and rather

than have a scene (which she was perfectly capable of creating) he talked to her in the judge's chambers. She had aged in these weeks, no question about that. She might even have learned something.

"You owe me a thousand dollars, Hewitt," she said.

"Oh no I don't! I had to take you in," he said.

"You know I'll get it anyway."

"But not from me."

"You almost called me 'Merle' then, didn't you?"

"Not as close as you thought."

Her small smile faded, and she looked away. "I suppose not. To you, I'm just not worth the trouble."

"You would be trouble, Merle. You would have to be won, conquered, disciplined. I could do it. It would have to be done over and over again, and I could do that too. But if I ever settle down to one woman, it will be one who solves more problems for me than she creates."

Now she did laugh. "Well, that's not me! One thing, I know myself now." Her face lost its glowing smile and looked old again. "No, there'll be no more fun for me. All the rest of my life, I'll pay for this."

"You weren't to blame for what he did, Merle. Each man makes that decision himself."

She looked him in the eye and said, "But I was with him when he did it. We have to share each other's sins too—all of us! I know that now. I'm not going to make Neil's life miserable any longer. But I want you to believe this, Mr. Hewitt—as long as I live, I'll know in my heart that I knew he did it, I knew he was capable of doing it, and I let it happen. And sometimes, just letting something happen is the worst sin of all."

"I believe you."

She smiled gratefully. "Thank you. Just for that, I'm going to do something nice for you. Don't ask what—you'll find out! Good-by, and thank you again. I learned a lot from you—even that hamhocks and beans are delicious, if you're hungry enough."

They shook hands. "Hamhocks and beans have always been favorites of mine," he said.

At the courthouse, the station agent was waiting for him. "You sure get a lot of telegrams, and you send a lot, too, Mr. Hewitt," he said. "Got another one for you."

"Afraid I live by telegrams," Hewitt said.

This one was from Colonel Auffenhaus, and it said:

DELIVER THEM PERSONALLY AND THEY GET FIVE WITH FIVE SUSPENDED STOP THEY MUST WORK STOP SQUAD-RON SLACK NEEDS DRILL STOP LOOK FORWARD SEEING YOU

"Hell!" said Hewitt. "I don't want to go to Fort Kearney."

"There's too much strain on this job for me," the agent was saying. "I'm quitting and moving to Texas. Maybe get a job with the Katy. Mrs. Patterson will take over. I dunno about a woman, but I hope for the best."

Hewitt tipped him ten dollars. The next morning, as he and Toby and Mac were boarding the southbound stage, with Rowdy tied on behind, a huge, burly man whose head and face were both smooth-shaven wept and insisted on kissing Hewitt's hand. His gratitude was more than he could express; all he could say was "Baa, baa, baa, baa!"

Hewitt got rid of him eventually. "He's so drunk he couldn't hit the ground with his hat in three throws," he said, climbing into the stage.

"Lucky stiff!" Toby said morosely. "Why don't you pay us that other hundred dollars, Mr. Hewitt?"

The long ride down to the Q, by stage. Then the U.P.,

switching back and forth, it seemed, forever, to get to Fort Kearney. He almost envied Toby and Mac, watching them slip back into the comfortable straitjacket of the Army, where life was shaped for you by *Regulations*.

The painful reunion with Max Auffenhaus. (They had never been friends—had not even liked each other.) Max would never learn to play poker if he lived to be a hundred, and he *would* play, and Hewitt owed him that much.

Even bad poker players have streaks, though, and sixteen hours later, Hewitt had to borrow back the one hundred dollars he had paid Toby and Mac. Colonel Auffenhaus now owned Rowdy. At least, Hewitt thought, yawning and rubbing his eyes on the side of his bed in Grand Island, he's good to a horse. About the only decent thing I can think to say about him. . . .

Whoever had been knocking on his door came back to try it once more. Hewitt got up in his underwear and stumbled to the door. He unlocked the chain and peered out, with due regard for decency.

It was a bellboy, with a telegram. "Shall I wait for an answer, sir?" he said.

Hewitt yawned again. "Yes, come on in while I read it. May have to answer it."

"Yes, sir. Some people live by telegrams, sir."

This one was from his partner Conrad Meuse in Cheyenne. It said:

SHIPPEY CHECK FOR NINE THOUSAND CLEARED BUT CAN-NOT UNDERSTAND YOUR EXPENSE ACCOUNT STOP WE MUST DISCUSS THIS IN DETAIL STOP INSIST YOU RETURN AT ONCE STOP ALSO WIRE DISPOSITION PACKAGE AR-RIVED FOR YOU FROM SODAK STOP APPEARS TO BE LIFE-SIZE OIL PAINTING STOP SHALL I OPEN IT AND GET IT APPRAISED FOR SALE

"There will be an answer," he said. He leaned on the dresser to write rapidly, while the bellboy waited:

DO NOT REPEAT DO NOT OPEN OR APPRAISE PACKAGE STOP LEAVING FOR CHEYENNE NEXT TRAIN WEST STOP HAVE PAINTING DELIVERED TO MY ROOM

ALL ABOUT
COIN
COLLECTING

by Ellen Weiss

illustrated by Chris Murphy

Reader's Digest Children's Books™

Many thanks to
Stephen L. Bobbitt, Barbara J. Gregory,
Robert W. Hoge, and Kelly Swett of the
American Numismatic Association for
reviewing the text and artwork
for this book.

Picture Credits: (t=top, b=bottom, m=middle, l=left,
r=right, c=center, F=Front, C=Cover, B=Back)
Courtesy of the Museum of the American Numismatic Association: 4l, 5bl, 9tr,
11tr, 11mr, 11br, 14ml, 16tl, 20tl, 22tl, 26tl, 27br, 29br; Courtesy of The
American Numismatic Society, New York: 7br; Mashantucket Pequot Museum
and Research Center: 8tl; Smithsonian Institution, NNC, Douglas Mudd: 9br, 22tr,
23br, 27tl; Courtesy of the U.S. Mint: Cbl, 4tl, 11tr, 12tl, 14ml, 16tl, 21tl, 28tl;
Photo from the Wooden Nickel Historical Museum, San Antonio, TX: 15tr.

Reader's Digest Children's Books
Reader's Digest Road, Pleasantville, NY 10570-7000
Manufactured in China.
ISBN: 1-57584-673-X
10 9 8 7 6 5 4 3 2 1

TABLE OF CONTENTS

How to Use...

COLLECTING COINS

Alexander the Great coin

1652 Louis XIV silver ecu

1806 Napolean franc

1924 Italian fascist lire

Massachusetts pine tree shilling

With the book and kit you have in your hands, you hold the key to an exciting new world—the world of coins and coin collecting. Until now, you may not have paid much attention to the coins that pass through your hands every day. But you could be missing pocketfuls of fun!

Why collect coins? There are all kinds of reasons. Maybe you've seen some cool foreign coins or collected a few quarters from the U.S. Mint's 50 State Quarters™ Program. But did you know that over time—if you choose coins carefully—they might go up in value? You could spend a little money on coins now and possibly end up with a collection that's worth more money when you're an adult. And—best of all—there's always the chance that you'll find something valuable right inside your pocket.

Did You Know?

The only person to assemble a complete collection of U.S. coins was Louis E. Eliasberg, Sr. In 1950, he bought the last piece he needed—a No Arrow-1873-CC Seated Liberty dime. It was the only one of its kind, and it cost him about $4,000. In 1996, the coin sold for $550,000.

It's a Free Country

You can spend any money ever made in the United States, no matter how old it is. So if you happen to have a 1944-D zinc-coated steel Lincoln cent, worth around $10,000, you can use it any time you're short a penny for bubble gum.

History on a Dime

Every coin is a little disk packed full of history, language, and geography. What country does the coin come from? When was it made? Who's that person on the coin? And what do all those Latin words mean?

If you become interested in coins and collecting, you'll find that you aren't alone. There are kids all over the world who collect coins. So, while you're having fun learning about coins, you can also make new friends who share your interest.

THE ORIGIN OF MONEY

The words "money" and "mint" come from Moneta, another name for the Roman goddess Juno. According to one popular story, it all started around 390 BC, when enemies attempted to sneak into Rome. But some noisy geese began flapping and squawking, and the invaders were caught. Because geese are sacred to Moneta, goddess of warning, the Romans built their mint in a shrine dedicated to her—and Moneta has been linked to coins ever since.

From Cows to Coins

Money is so common we don't think about it much—except when we need a quarter to buy a piece of candy. But what did people do before money was invented?

Let's say Harry had a herd of cows and Letitia had a large piece of woven cloth. If Harry wanted to make a shirt and Letitia wanted a cow, they could trade, or barter. But what if Letitia didn't want a cow, or Harry thought the cloth was only worth a quarter of a cow?

This is where money comes in. Anything can be money, as long as everybody agrees it is. Let's say there are lots of

Worth His Salt!

Salt is important stuff. It preserves food for long periods without refrigeration. Salt is needed by the human body. And it tastes good! That's why, through the centuries, salt has often been used as money.

Anything Goes!

Almost anything you can think of has been used as money somewhere in the world. For centuries, the Pacific islanders of Yap used flat stone disks. They ran a pole through a hole carved in the center of each disk so they could carry their money around and trade it for anything from land to brides. The largest disks measured 12 feet across and weighed 2 tons. Their main role must have been to impress the neighbors!

buttons in Letitia's town. People decide that a yard of cloth is worth 20 buttons, while a cow is worth 100. Harry has 100 buttons that he got from Francine, who needed a cow. He gives 20 of them to Letitia for the cloth. Then Letitia uses her 20 buttons to buy some bananas, cheese, and a jug of olive oil.

Over time, people make the system better. They agree that big buttons will be worth more than little buttons, so they don't have to carry around so many buttons.

Think of the change in your pocket as being like those buttons. When the U.S. government makes money, it ensures that all the dimes are worth 10 cents, all the quarters are worth 25 cents, and so forth. Our government guarantees the value of our currency.

Early Coins

The first stamped metal coins were made in ancient Lydia, part of modern-day Turkey, around 650 BC. Workers took pieces of electrum, a mixture of gold and silver found in nature, and stamped them with a lion's head, the symbol of Lydia's king. The idea of using coins spread to Greece and, later, through the Roman Empire to the rest of Europe. China, meanwhile, was working on its own system of money. Some scholars believe the Chinese used coins even earlier than the Lydians.

Greek coin (525-500 BC)
(front)   (back)

Roman coin
(after 211 BC)

Lydian coin
(600-570 BC)

wampum belt

quahog shell

EARLY AMERICAN MONEY

Before the first European settlers landed in the New World in the 1600s, native Americans in the Northeast strung together beads made from seashells, called wampum. Strings and belts made of these beads were used as symbolic gifts to mark treaties, ceremonies, and special occasions.

When the Europeans arrived, they realized wampum was perfect for trading. Dutch settlers began making huge amounts of beads out of glass and shells to use as currency. Indians also began to exchange wampum for goods. Purple beads were worth double the white ones.

Early Americans also used local products as money. In the colonies of Virginia and Maryland, tobacco leaves were bundled and traded for food or guns. In Massachusetts, the "money" was often furs or fish.

Thanks, Tom!
The gentleman on the front of the nickel is the third president of the United States, Thomas Jefferson. A very smart fellow, he was largely responsible for figuring out how American money would work.

Thanks, Ben!

The first U.S. coin is often called the Fugio cent (here, Fugio means "time flies"). The coin says WE ARE ONE and MIND YOUR BUSINESS—fitting mottoes for a new country. These words were written by Benjamin Franklin, who was fond of giving helpful advice to his countrymen.

obverse

reverse

Dollars and Cents

As the colonies grew, coins and paper money developed in a haphazard way. Each colony produced its own currency. Because the colonies were under British rule, they minted coins in British units—pounds, shillings, and pence. This also made trade with British merchants easier.

During the American Revolution, the colonies issued money to help pay for the war. They printed paper dollars, called continentals. But times were difficult for the rebels. Troops were hungry and ill-clothed. There wasn't much around to buy and the continentals were worth very little, so soldiers used them to line their boots.

When the war was over, the United States of America needed its own money. In 1792, the Congress passed a Mint Act establishing the dollar, worth 100 cents, as the basic unit of money. The following year, the new U.S. Mint in Philadelphia produced its first coins for circulation—11,178 shiny copper cents.

North and South

During the Civil War, the southern states broke away from the Union and issued their own money. Montgomery, Alabama was established as the capital of the Confederate States of America. Although confederate money is not very valuable today, many people like to collect it for its historical interest.

confederate currency

MODERN U.S. COINS

By law, all modern U.S. coins must have certain features. The words UNITED STATES OF AMERICA appear on every coin. On the front side (obverse), the coins state LIBERTY. On the back (reverse), the eagle insignia is required on all coins worth over 10 cents, except for the new 50 State Quarters. If the eagle is present, the motto E PLURIBUS UNUM ("one out of many") must also appear. Since 1938, all coins say IN GOD WE TRUST.

Modern Materials

Over time, there have been changes in the materials used to make U.S. coins. The U.S. Mint must produce coins for less than their face value. In other words, a nickel has to cost less than five cents to make. As precious metals have become scarcer and more expensive, the U.S. Mint has had to use cheaper substitutes. In 1792, all U.S. coins were made of gold, silver, or copper. But by 1933, gold had become too costly. In 1965, the U.S. Mint stopped using silver in quarters and dimes—they are now made of copper and nickel. One-cent pieces are made of copper-plated zinc.

Honest Abe
Abraham Lincoln is the only president on a United States coin who faces right.

Celebrating Women

The first real (non-mythological) woman to appear on a circulating U.S. coin was Susan B. Anthony, a feminist leader who worked to obtain the right to vote for women. The dollar coin was introduced in 1979, but people confused it with the quarter and spent it by accident. After two years, the Susan B. Anthony dollar was discontinued.

Susan B. Anthony dollar

In 2000, the government introduced a new dollar coin honoring Sacajawea, the young Shoshone Indian woman who helped the explorers Lewis and Clark make their way across the American West.

Sacajawea dollar

Coin Design Today

The coins we use most frequently are the cent, nickel, dime, and quarter. This century, there have been few changes in these coins. Between 1913 and 1938, nickels had a portrait of a native American on the front and a buffalo—the American bison—on the back. Today, the nickel shows Thomas Jefferson on the front and his home, Monticello, on the back. Until 1959, the back of the cent featured sheaves of wheat. It was changed to the Lincoln Memorial to honor the 150th anniversary of President Lincoln's birth.

Buffalo nickel

Lincoln cent

Roosevelt dime

Since 1946, Franklin Delano Roosevelt has been portrayed on the front of the dime. President Roosevelt, who served from 1933 to 1945, suffered from polio—then a common, crippling illness. He founded an organization called the March of Dimes, that still remains dedicated to the eradication of polio and other childhood diseases. In 1976, a new quarter was issued to commemorate the Bicentennial, the 200th birthday of our country. And now, the 50 State Quarters are rolling off the Mint's presses.

Bicentennial quarter

The U.S. Mint doesn't produce coins just for circulation. It also makes commemorative coins, which celebrate important people, places, institutions, and events.

Coin commemorating the U.S. Constitution

50 NEW QUARTERS!

In the mid-1990s, Congress decided it was time for our country to have some new quarters. On December 1, 1997, President Clinton signed the 50 States Commemorative Coin Program Act. The new quarters will honor each state with a unique design on the back of the state's quarter. The coins are being issued in the same order as the states became part of the United States of America. Since five new designs will make their debut every year, the program will take 10 years to complete.

Our National Heritage

When lawmakers in Congress created the program, they were not just thinking about new coins; they were also thinking about American children. They wanted to help kids learn about the states, about "their history and geography, and the rich diversity of the national heritage." They were also hoping to find a way to encourage kids to collect coins. "It is appropriate," states the act, "to launch a commemorative circulating coin program that encourages young people and their families to collect memorable tokens of all the States for the face value of the coins."

A Pile of Change
Over the course of the 50 State Quarters Program, the U.S. Mint will produce between 500 million and just over 1 billion quarters for each state.

The 50 State Quarters Program marks the first time in history that there will be 50 designs for one coin denomination, and the new quarters have attracted the attention of adults as well as children. In fact, the U.S. Mint has had to make many extra coins of all denominations, because people are saving so many of the new quarters instead of spending them.

50 New Designs

Who's designing the quarters? Well, it could be you! If your state's quarter design isn't finished yet, the U.S. Mint designers may be busy gathering ideas right now.

Here's how it works. The governor of each state chooses three to five good ideas and submits them to the U.S. Mint. Your governor's office will have details on how to submit ideas for your state. On the U.S. Mint's website (see p. 31), you'll find a large template of a blank coin for sketching out your designs, as well as a list of rules about what can and can't be featured on the new quarters.

Once a state has submitted its favorite ideas, the U.S. Mint designers produce artwork for each one. The artwork is reviewed by experts, revised, and sent to the Secretary of the Treasury for approval. The approved artwork is sent to the governor for the state to select one piece. This piece is then returned to the Secretary of the Treasury for final approval.

How to Use the 50 State Quarters Coin Collector Map and Checklist

The map in your kit shows each state and its capital city. At the bottom, you'll find the states listed in the order that they joined the Union. As you collect each quarter in the 50 State Quarters Program, place the "Got It!" sticker on the appropriate state on the map and check off the name of the state on the list below.

How to Use the Official 50 State Quarters Coin Folder

Use the coin folder to store and display your quarter collection. The slots are organized alphabetically by state name. Slip each quarter into its slot as soon as you collect it. The extra flap of paper will protect your coins from damage.

THE U.S. MINT

Since it was created in 1792, the U.S. Mint has been our national factory for coins, our only official money until the Civil War. At that time, the Bureau of Engraving and Printing began making paper money, or "greenbacks," as everybody took to calling them. Today, the Bureau churns out over 9 billion notes per year at its sites in Washington, DC, and Fort Worth, TX.

Coins, Coins, Coins

The U.S. Mint makes coins—lots and lots and lots of them—at its two main locations in Philadelphia, PA, and Denver, CO. (There are smaller mints in West Point, NY, and San Francisco, CA, but only special coins are made there.) You can usually tell where a coin was made by its mint mark—a tiny letter *P* or *D*. However, all cents made in Philadelphia and all other coins made there before 1979 (except 1942–45 nickels) do not carry mint marks. The number of coins rolling out of the Philadelphia and Denver mints is staggering. Billions of pennies, nickels, dimes, and quarters come tumbling out of the coin

Phony as a Four-cent Piece

Counterfeit coins imitate rare and valuable ones. The toughest fakes to spot are struck, or stamped out, from counterfeit dies made illegally from genuine coins. But this counterfeiting process reproduces all the same imperfections—tiny lumps of metal, small hollows—of the original, genuine coin.

Don't Take Any Wooden Nickels!

You might be surprised to hear that wooden money was produced in the 1930s, at the time of the Great Depression. During a cash shortage, two towns in Washington state decided to make wooden currency until the emergency was over.

wooden money

presses each year and begin their journey to the pockets and piggy banks of America.

From Mint to Bank to You

How do the coins get to you? The U.S. Mint loads them onto trucks and dispatches them to the twelve Federal Reserve banks around the country. The Federal Reserve system is our nation's independent central bank. It acts as a bank for banks. One of its jobs is to distribute the currency made by the U.S. Mint and the Bureau of Engraving and Printing, both part of the U.S. Treasury Department. After the money travels from these two agencies to the Federal Reserve banks, it is bought by local banks across the country.

Why does the Treasury need to keep making new money all the time? Why don't the coins and bills keep going around and around forever, from buyer to seller, employer to worker? It's because all those hands wear the money out. Dollar bills, for instance, last about 18 months before they become worn. When a bank receives old bills, it returns them in bundles to the Federal Reserve banks, where they're shredded. In return, the bank stocks up on new bills. Coins last longer than bills, but eventually they wear out, too. Banks also return coins to the Federal Reserve, which returns them to the U.S. Mint, where they are melted down to make new coins.

To decide how many coins to make each year, the U.S. Mint does "coinage forecasting." Its experts monitor our economy, watching the number of coins in circulation during heavy spending times such as the winter holidays. It is not an accurate science, so estimates must be broad enough to make sure there are always enough coins around.

HOW DO THEY MAKE

Once you start looking at coins, you'll notice that both sides of each coin are beautifully decorated. This artwork is produced by trained sculptor-engravers. But how does the art get onto the coins?

1.
The artist draws the design for a new coin on paper.

2.
She sculpts the design—with all its tiny details—in clay that has been pressed into a large plaster basin.

3.
When the model is finished, the artist pours a mixture of wet plaster into the mold. When the plaster hardens, it is removed, producing a negative model. The artist then carves letters and numbers into it…backwards! She presses Silly Putty into the letters to check her work—the words read normally on the putty.

4.
Now the artist brushes the plaster mold with liquid soap and pours wet plaster into it. When the plaster hardens, presto—out it pops, thanks to the soap.

5.
The plaster cast must be sent to Washington for approval. Before it leaves, a rubber negative mold is made—just in case somebody drops the plaster one!

COINS, ANYWAY?

6.

Now the artist makes a model from the rubber negative using epoxy, a very hard plastic. Finally, it's time to make the metal coin.

7.

In the transfer engraving room, the art is transferred from model size to coin size by precision machines about 100 years old. The needle to the right moves very slowly over the epoxy model, recording every change in its surface. The carving needle on the left side moves the same way, gradually inscribing the design into a small steel cylinder, called the master hub. The master hub will be used only two or three times, but is the great-grandparent of the millions and millions of coins that will be made from it. Let's see how.

master hub

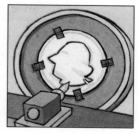

epoxy model

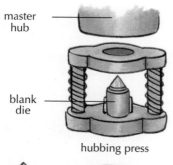

master hub

blank die

hubbing press

8.

In the hubbing room, a powerful hydraulic press squeezes the design from the master hub onto the master dies—four-inch bullet-shaped lengths of steel cut from long cylinders—and flattens out the pointy end of the dies as it goes. Then, working hubs are made from the master dies, and working dies are made from these. The working dies will stamp out the coins. One working die can make 300,000 quarters or a million pennies (the metal that pennies are made of is softer, so the dies don't wear out as fast).

blank die   master hub

finished master die

9.

It's finally time to start cutting blanks. The metal arrives at the U.S. Mint in huge coiled sheets. For half-dollars, quarters, and dimes, the metal sheet is put together like a sandwich: pure copper in the middle, and a mixture, or alloy, of copper and nickel on the outside. Nickels are made of that same copper-nickel alloy straight through—one huge roll of alloy yields 325,000 nickels. The metal sheets are fed through a blanking press—sort of a giant cookie cutter. The coin-making room is so noisy that everybody wears earplugs. The blanks move along the production line. The leftover metal from the sheets is shredded and recycled.

10.

The blanks are heated in a huge furnace to soften them and are then washed and given a cold-water bath.

11.

The next stop is the upsetting machine, which "upsets" the blanks by adding a raised rim, or edge, around each coin. This edge is harder than the rest of the coin, which helps in the striking process.

plain blank

blank with upset edge

12.

The coining press is a huge, loud machine that strikes the blanks, whacking the design onto them. It is the working dies (see step 8), fixed to the stamping arm (hammer) and platform (anvil) of the press, that shape each coin. A fast coining press can turn out 12 coins per second. If these are half-dollars, quarters, or dimes, they sit in special grooved collars as they're stamped. Each coin is squeezed outward into the collar, which forms grooves, or reeds, in the coin rim.

hammer   anvil

13.

When the coins come spewing out of the press, they're hot. A press operator spot-checks them with a magnifying glass to make sure the designs are perfect. If not, she rejects them.

14.

Finally, the coins are machine-counted and bagged. Cents go into $50 bags and dimes into $1,000 bags about the same size. The bags are stacked up on shelves, ready to be loaded into the unmarked tractor-trailer trucks that will take them to the Federal Reserve banks.

COIN COLLECTING: READY, SET, GO!

One of the great things about coin collecting is that it's very easy to start. You can begin a collection with the coins you have in your house right now.

Coin collecting is a hobby that connects people all over the world. Kids can trade information and coins with kids from other countries—especially over the Internet. Both the Boy Scouts and Girl Scouts of America offer a coin-collecting badge. There are coin collections in museums around the world, as well as international meetings devoted to coin collecting. There are societies to join, both faraway and near home, and there are special clubs and publications just for kids. Generally, adults interested in numismatics—the science and history of money—are very interested in helping the next generation of coin collectors get started.

Starting Your Collection

You can be as serious as you like about collecting. You may just want to keep a few interesting coins in an old peanut-butter jar. But if you want to use the Internet and the library to gather more information, there's no limit to what you can learn. (See p. 31 for ideas about where to begin.) The first thing to do is read as much as you can. The more you know about coins, the better prepared you'll be to make your first coin purchases.

Once you're armed with information, where do you find coins to collect? The U.S. Mint is a good place to start. The Mint offers proof sets—specially minted, extra-shiny, extra-fancy versions of the coins that are produced each year. If you write to the U.S. Mint, they'll add you to their mailing list of millions of collectors.

What's on a Coin?

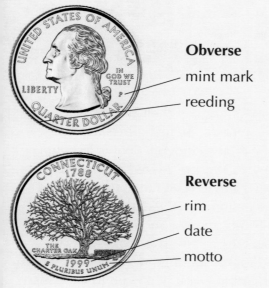

Obverse
— mint mark
— reeding

Reverse
— rim
— date
— motto

Asking adult friends and relatives to help you find the coins you're looking for is another way to build a collection, especially if you're trying to assemble a full set of coins from a particular year, like the year you were born. And coin dealers are usually happy to spend time with new collectors and offer suggestions for inexpensive coins that are fun to own.

How to Use the Magnifying Glass

A magnifying glass is a useful piece of equipment for all serious coin collectors. It allows you to see details you wouldn't notice otherwise. Tiny nicks, scratches, and worn places will all affect the value of a coin. Other details are also fun to spot. Use your magnifying glass to look at the picture of the Lincoln Memorial on the back of a penny. See the tiny figure sitting inside? It's Honest Abe himself.

Lincoln cent

How to Use the Commemorative Coin Set

Make a cool collector's item! Choose as a theme the year of your birth or some other major event. Find a coin of each denomination—cent, nickel, dime, quarter—from that year. Write your name in the space provided and use the other lines for important information, such as mint mark and coin condition. If you like, you can give the coin set to a friend— just fill in his or her name instead of yours.

Commemorative
Coin Set

Taiwanese bill

Chinese coin

MONEY FROM OTHER COUNTRIES

money from the former U.S.S.R.

Japanese money

Money expresses people's pride in their history, leaders, and economy. One of the first things a new country does when it becomes independent is to begin making its own money, just as the United States did. Different countries design their own money in different ways, as shown in the pictures on these two pages.

Unlike the United States, many countries print paper money in various colors and sizes. This makes it easy to tell the bills apart and makes them fun to collect as well.

If you visit another country, you will need to exchange some of your American money for the money of the country you are visiting. In Japan, for example, you can only use Japanese yen; in Mexico, Mexican pesos are the official currency.

Collecting Foreign Money

With so many attractive coins and bills available, you might enjoy starting a collection of foreign currency.

money from the Czech Republic

Making Money
Want to make a color copy of a dollar bill? Better not copy it exactly—it's against the law. You can make color or black-and-white copies, as long as they are 25% smaller or 50% larger than the real bill.

Australian money

Yemeni money

Indian money

Often, the easiest way to begin is by talking to people—family, friends, teachers, neighbors—who have traveled recently to other countries. Try asking them for any extra change they may have brought back. You can also buy coin sets from the mints of many countries, often at a low price. The Internet is another good place to start exploring. (There is a list of web sites where you can learn more about U.S. and foreign money on p. 31.) Once you have collected a few coins, you can begin trading your extras with friends who may have money from completely different countries.

new European money—the euro

Nigerian money

Kenyan money

Egyptian money

TaKiNG CaRe OF YoUR COINS

You don't need any fancy equipment to begin your coin collection. If you're starting off with coins that aren't valuable, you can handle them casually and keep them in any convenient place. After all, they were jingling around in people's pockets long before they reached you. But if you become interested in rarer coins, you'll need to be more careful about how you handle them. For example, serious coin collectors never pick up a coin by the flat sides. They always hold it by the rim, because even finger marks can lower the value of a coin. It's considered very rude to pick up someone's coin by the flat sides!

Cleaning Coins

How you clean your coins also depends on their value. Coin experts will tell you never to clean a coin, period. Because rare coins are scrutinized closely under magnifying glasses, even the tiniest mark or scratch will be noticeable—and almost anything can scratch a coin. But if you want to clean coins that aren't particularly special, you don't have to be as careful.

Non-cents!
American coin collectors never use the word "penny," which comes from the British money system. In the United States, these coins are called "cents."

Try using a soft, old toothbrush to clean your coins. Clean dirt out of crevices with a toothpick or a plastic pen top. Or, you can wipe coins clean with a cotton ball moistened with rubbing alcohol. But remember—don't clean important coins. And never use metal polish, or a brush that's stiff or made of wire—these can damage even ordinary coins.

Storing Coins

Soon, you'll need to store your growing collection. An important tip on storage—don't use flexible plastic envelopes to hold your coins. Over the years, collectors have discovered that chemicals in the plastic (PVCs) break down, making a sticky mess that gums up the coins. Another big coin-destroyer is the acid found in cheap paper. The best material for storing valuable coins is acid-free paper. You can buy little envelopes made of acid-free paper at coin shops. Cardboard coin-collecting books are fine for coins that aren't very valuable. Today, many coins are sold in sealed plastic blocks, or "slabs," that protect them from damage.

How to Make the Coin Record Keeper

1. First, decide how you would like to organize your coins. Coins are usually grouped by denomination, from smallest to largest, and by date, from oldest to newest.

2. Now you're ready to record your first coin. Open the record keeper provided in your kit. Place the coin under the page, at least one-half inch above the coin label lines.

3. Place the coin ring over the page and press down lightly to hold your coin in place. Rub a colored pencil back and forth over the top of the coin until the image appears.

4. Working carefully, record the date, mint mark, and denomination of your coin on the label lines. Add any other important notes.

HOW MUCH ARE YOUR COINS WORTH?

Coin collecting is fun, but for some people it's also a way to invest money—a bit like the stock market. If you buy a coin for ten dollars now, it may be worth $30 some years down the road. But, like the stock market, the coin market has its ups and downs. You can't count on coins making money.

So...How Much?

Many factors determine a coin's value. The first thing to remember is that coins are valued by their scarcity, not by their age. If someone gives you a silver dollar from the 1800s, you might think, *Wow! This must be worth a lot!* But since there are many silver dollars around from the 1800s, it might not be worth much more than a plain old dollar. If small quantities of a particular coin were produced, however, the value of each one skyrockets.

1885 silver dollar

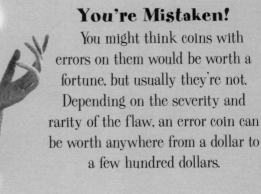

You're Mistaken!

You might think coins with errors on them would be worth a fortune, but usually they're not. Depending on the severity and rarity of the flaw, an error coin can be worth anywhere from a dollar to a few hundred dollars.

Brasher doubloon

Super Seven

One of the most famous rare American coins—the Brasher doubloon—was made in 1787. A goldsmith named Ephraim Brasher wanted to win a contract to make copper coins for New York state. To impress the officials, he made some sample $16 coins in gold. Though Brasher's designs were not chosen, the seven known Brasher doubloons are among the most valuable coins in the world—worth about $1 million apiece!

Making the Grade

Several other factors contribute to coin value. These include the current values of the coin market, the actual value of the metal in the coin, and—most importantly—the condition of the coin. That's why collectors and dealers are so careful about how they handle coins.

There are 11 grades of uncirculated, or "Mint State," coins, depending on what condition they're in. After these come circulated coins, with several grades of their own. The lowest collectible grade is called About Good, which actually means pretty bad! These coins are not usually worth much at all.

About Good coin

Proof It!

The U.S. Mint makes the special, extra-shiny coins known as proofs just for collectors. They are struck two or more times on highly polished coin blanks. The designs are frosted for contrast and show perfect detail. After striking, the coins are removed carefully from the press and packaged to protect their mirrorlike surfaces.

proof coin

JUMP START:

You don't have to visit a coin dealer to find coins that are worth extra money. America's pockets, drawers, and coffee cans are full of coins, some of which are valuable. Here are a few examples:

1.

Several thousand cent coins made in 1955 have an error on them: the date and lettering on the "heads" side are doubled, giving them a ghosted look. These "doubled-die" pennies are worth about $400 each even in used condition. The same thing happened to some 1972 pennies, which can be worth from $50 to $200. It happened again in 1995—you can spot ghosting on the word "LIBERTY." These coins are worth about $40.

2.

In 1960, some cent coins made in San Francisco had dates that were just a bit smaller than normal. These "small date" cents are worth about $20 each now, but they're sitting in sugar bowls all over the country. You can spot the smaller dates because the top of the "6" is exactly lined up with the top of the "0."

3.

Since 1980, a small letter *P* has been stamped on all coins made in Philadelphia, except the cent. Before that, the Philadelphia coins were identifiable because they had no mint mark. But in 1982, dimes that were supposed to have the *P* didn't. If you find one of these, you'll make at least $25.

VALUABLE COINS YOU COULD ACTUALLY FIND iN YOUR POCKET

4.

The *P* mint mark disappeared again from a batch of quarters made in Philadelphia in 1989. These coins are worth about $40.

5.

In 1965, the U.S. Mint stopped using silver in quarters and dimes because it was too expensive. But a few quarters slipped through. If you find a 1965 quarter without the copper-colored line around the rim, you've got something pretty valuable.

6.

In 1964, some nickels were struck in Denver with a defective die. Instead of saying E PLURIBUS UNUM, they say E PLURIDUS UNUM. The coins aren't worth much, but it's fun to spot a silly-looking mistake like that.

7.

Once in a great while, a coin will be "overstruck"—that is, struck over an image that's already there. These coins can be worth a lot. A 1973 nickel that was overstruck with a 1974 one sold for $1,650 at auction.

8.

During World War II, the government needed to save money and metal for weapons and ammunition. Many unusual coins made during that period are worth a good deal of money now. Take, for example, a particular dime made in 1942. To save money on dies, the U.S. Mint's technicians decided simply to change the date on the 1941 die—they cut a "2" right over the "1." But it didn't work very well, and the dimes were quickly taken out of circulation. If you find one in your uncle's shoe box, it could be worth about $16,000!

COLLECTING AND CONNECTING

Coin collecting can be a solitary hobby or a great way to connect with other people. On p. 31, you'll find a list of coin clubs to join. Or you can start one of your own right where you live. Even collecting and trading coins with one or two other kids is fun.

Your school might already have a coin collecting club. If not, you could probably find a teacher who'd be willing to help you start one. Or you can simply start a club yourself. Ask permission to put up signs at school or at a community center, and see if any fellow coin lovers respond. Talk to friends about coins, too. Even if they're not already interested in the subject, your enthusiasm will probably rub off as they find out how much fun you're having.

Party, Party, Party

Another idea is to have a coin party. Pile up coins for everybody to look at and invite friends to bring coins from their homes, too. Have a coin guidebook available so you can all look up the coins and see if you've found anything special. You can also set out materials for making rubbings.

Coins can keep you occupied—during long car trips, while waiting for your mom or dad to finish an errand, or when visiting relatives. You can also ask your family or friends to let you inspect their pocket change. What's the oldest coin they have? While on a trip, which mint marks are you seeing more of? Which of the 50 State Quarters have you spotted? You may make some interesting discoveries!

SOURCES AND RESOURCES

Organizations

National coin-collecting organizations are happy to help new collectors get started. They'll send you materials and help you hook up with regional, state, or local coin clubs.

American Numismatic Association
818 North Cascade Avenue
Colorado Springs, CO 80903-3279
www.money.org

The American Numismatic Society
140 William Street
New York, NY 10038-3801
www.amnumsoc.org

Canadian Numismatic Association
P.O. Box 226
Barrie, Ontario, L4M 4T2, Canada
www.nunetcan.net/cna.htm

Books

There are loads and loads of good books about coins. You can find some of them at your library—and coin dealers and bookstores will have others. Here are just a handful of good ones.

Coin Collector's Survival Manual.
Scott A. Travers. Chicago: Bonus Books, 1996

Coin World Almanac. Coin World Editors. Sidney, OH: Amos Press, 1990

A Guide Book of United States Coins.
R.S. Yeoman. New York: Golden Books, annual

The Handbook of United States Coins.
R.S. Yeoman. New York: Golden Books, annual

The Whitman Coin Guide to Coin Collecting. Kenneth Bresset. New York: St. Martin's Press, 1999

Magazines and Newspapers

Coin World (weekly)
P.O. Box 150
Sidney, OH 45365

Numismatic News (weekly)
700 E. State Street
Iola, WI 54990

COINage Magazine (monthly)
4880 Market Street
Ventura, CA 93003

Coins Magazine (monthly)
700 E. State Street
Iola, WI 54990

The Numismatist (monthly)
American Numismatic Association
818 North Cascade Avenue
Colorado Springs, CO 80903-3279

Appearing twice a year in
The Numismatist: First Strike
(for young numismatists)

The Internet

The U.S. Mint has a very interesting web site—http://www.usmint.gov. On this site, you can find out more about the history of the U.S. Mint, the 50 State Quarters Program, and many other subjects. You can click on a whole section just for kids, called H.I.P. Pocket Change. It has lots of information and fun activities, like a musical crayon box that lets you design your own coins while playing sounds.

In addition to the three web sites listed above (under Organizations), the following web sites contain useful information and links:

    www.calgarycoin.com
    www.coinshows.com/yp.html
    www.coin-universe.com
    www.coinworld.com
    www.telesphere.com/ts/coins
    www.coinlibrary.com

COINING WORDS:
A GLOSSARY OF COIN TERMS

alloy: a mixture of two or more metals

blank: a metal disk ready to be made into a coin by stamping (see **planchet**)

Buffalo nickel: the Indian Head five-cent piece, minted between 1913 and 1938

colonials: coins issued by the 13 colonies before the Declaration of Independence

commemorative: special coin issued by a mint to honor a person, organization, or event

denomination: the face value of a series of coins or bills, such as 1 cent, 5 cents, 10 cents, 25 cents

device: the main elements of the design of a coin

die: engraved piece made of hard metal used to stamp, or strike, the design onto the softer metal of a coin

doubled die: die that creates more than one image when striking a coin

electrum: naturally-occurring alloy of gold and silver that was used in ancient coins

error: coin containing a mistake made during minting

legend: an inscription on a coin

mint mark: a symbol or letter that tells you at which mint the coin was manufactured

mint set: a set of uncirculated coins sold by a mint. It includes one of each denomination of coin produced in a particular year.

motto: a phrase that expresses an important idea, like In God We Trust

numismatics: the study and collection of objects used as money

numismatist: a person who is an expert in numismatics

obverse: the "heads" side of a coin; the side with the main design

planchet: a metal disk ready to be made into a coin by stamping (see **blank**)

proof: a specially-struck coin, made by a mint for collectors

Red Book: a popular name for *A Guide Book of United States Coins*. This book is the standard reference book for looking up coin prices and information.

reeding: the grooves around the rim of certain coins

reverse: the back, or "tails," side of a coin

rim: the raised border around the edge of a coin

series: coins of the same design, denomination, and type

uncirculated coins: coins that have never been used